Gertrude C. Pleasant

Books by ROBERT NATHAN

NOVELS *The Color of Evening* (1960)
So Love Returns (1958)
The Rancho of the Little Loves (1956)
Sir Henry (1955)
The Train in the Meadow (1953)
The Innocent Eve (1951)
The Married Look (1950)
The Adventures of Tapiola (1950, containing *Journey of Tapiola*, 1938, and *Tapiola's Brave Regiment*, 1941)
The River Journey (1949)
Long after Summer (1948)
Mr. Whittle and the Morning Star (1947)
But Gently Day (1943)
The Sea-Gull Cry (1942)
They Went On Together (1941)
Portrait of Jennie (1940)
Winter in April (1938)
The Barly Fields (1938, containing *The Fiddler in Barly*, 1926, *The Woodcutter's House*, 1927, *The Bishop's Wife*, 1928, *The Orchid*, 1931, and *There Is Another Heaven*, 1929)
The Enchanted Voyage (1936)
Road of Ages (1935)
One More Spring (1933)
Jonah (1925)

POEMS *The Green Leaf* (1950)
The Darkening Meadows (1945)
Morning in Iowa (1944)
Dunkirk (1941)
A Winter Tide (1940)
Selected Poems (1935)

THEATER *Jezebel's Husband & The Sleeping Beauty* (1953)
NON-FICTION *Journal for Josephine* (1943)
FOR YOUNG PEOPLE *The Snowflake and the Starfish* (1959)

These are BORZOI BOOKS, published in New York by ALFRED A. KNOPF, INC.

THE COLOR OF EVENING

THE COLOR
OF
EVENING

BY

ROBERT NATHAN

NEW YORK
Alfred · A · Knopf
1960

L. C. catalog card number: 60–8404

© ROBERT NATHAN, 1960

THIS IS A BORZOI BOOK,

PUBLISHED BY ALFRED A. KNOPF, INC.

FIRST EDITION

The sonnet *Be Not Afraid*, originally published in A WINTER TIDE, is taken from the sequence "Autumn Sonnets" in THE GREEN LEAF, *The Collected Poems of Robert Nathan*, published by Alfred A. Knopf, Inc. Copyright 1937, 1940, 1950 by Robert Nathan.

TO MY FRIEND

Bill Koshland

Be not afraid because the sun goes down;
It brings the sunset and the plover's cry.
Before the colors of the evening drown,
The stars will make new colors in the sky.
Night is no enemy. She passes by,
And shows us silence for our own heart's good;
For while we sleep, the roses multiply,
The little tree grows taller in the wood.
Fear not the night; the morning follows soon.
Each has his task to make the earth more fair.
It is by these, by midnight and by noon,
That she grows riper and her orchards bear.
Her fields would wither in a sun too bright;
They need the darkness too. Fear not the night.

I do not know (and have never known) anyone named Max Loeb, Hermione Bloemendal, Halys Smith, or Jon Kuzik. But there are millions and millions of people in the world, and for all I know, there may be a painter somewhere named Max Loeb who has led a blameless life, is married, and doesn't agree with me about music, poetry, or art. This is to tell him that there is no use suing me: I am innocent.

RN

THE COLOR OF EVENING

CHAPTER 1

SOUTH of Santa Monica along the shore stretch the ocean beaches, from Venice and Ocean Park to Palos Verdes, from Huntington and Long Beach to Newport and San Diego. Among them, between Venice and El Segundo, is the Playa del Rey, which is the only beach fitted for fires; the round fireplaces made of concrete rings dimple the sand to the north and to the south like raindrops on a lake. There at night the fires burn yellow and bright in the blue, sea-evening air; families bend over their cooking, children play, and couples wander in and out of shadow and firelight, up and down and across the sand, or lie together near the flames, screened by a blanket against the night wind from the sea. Behind them the ocean tumbles and darkens on the shore, the last green sunset light fades into stars; before them and around them the fires flare, and beyond them across the ocean highway the sea-gazing houses dream on their cliff. Over them the planes from the airport pass in rolling thunder and swim out over the beach like whales, blinking their red and green lights in the dusk, lifting, turning in higher circles to the east, or winking out over the Pacific on their way to the islands—to Hawaii, Guam, the Philippines, Japan.

Many nights in summer in the months of July and August and on through October the old painter Max Loeb came to the Playa del Rey with a few bits of wood for a fire picked up here and there, to cook his sausages or to warm a pot of beans, to look at the night sky and the beach with its dancing fires and the slanting come-and-go of arrowy shapes around him, studying to put it all down on canvas someday, when he found out how to do it. How to paint the evening air with its shadow and shine . . . to show how people looked, how the beach looked, in the year 1959, not to the new men (he had no use for most of them), but to Max Loeb.

There was no hurry, there was still plenty of time—maybe fifteen years, maybe twenty—without a heart attack, that is to say, or an obstruction.

Meanwhile, for the last five years he had rented a studio from Mrs. Bloemendal in Santa Monica, less than three miles away. This room, this studio, which was also his home, was simply the garage at the back of Mrs. Bloemendal's house; from it in the morning when he got up he could see the ocean at the bottom of the street blue as a Zuni bracelet, or in the evening, when his work was finished for the day, the sunset green and gold across the shining water. A bougainvillia vine grew along one side of the house, and a mock orange and a flowering Pittosporum gave a sweet orange-blossom smell to the air in spring. In summer the night-blooming jasmine filled the air with its bananalike fragrance, slightly rotten and disturbing.

The garage had a door, windows, a skylight, an old-fashioned icebox, a gas ring to cook on, and a small bathroom without a tub, put there by Mr. Bloemendal, who had been in the building trades; the bathtub itself was in the main house, across a small stone patio bordered by a few dusty plants. The rent was low because Mr. Loeb was an artist, and because Mrs. Bloemendal was lonely.

She was a tall, erect woman, still dark-haired (with a little gray in it), with a sincere but simple mind, and an innocent heart. She had been a show girl once, long ago, before she married Mr. Bloemendal; her name had been Minnie—Hermione—Riley then. She had no illusions about her career, but it left her with a feeling for the arts.

She had posed for Mr. Loeb two or three times; each time she came to the garage prepared to be at least a figure, classically draped, but all he ever wanted was the face. She didn't understand it; she had never been remarkable for her face. To old Max Loeb, however, faces were history. "Figures tell you nothing," he said. "From a nude without a head, you get no information."

"There is a face," he went on, "the portrait of a young woman, in the museum downtown, painted by an Italian of the Florentine school, maybe in the late fifteenth century. Not an important painter at all; I forget his name. But when I look at this girl, I actually see her; she is real to me, like somebody right here in Ocean Park, only better looking. And all of a sudden I understand the history of Florence, of Mantua, of Verona, just as if I were there. . . . It is the same sometimes in front of an El Greco, or a Holbein: history, you look at history in someone's face."

"So that's what you're after," said Mrs. Bloemendal, and examined herself in the glass. After a while she sighed, and touched her slightly wrinkled cheeks with her fingers already freckled with age. Was that really history, what she saw there?

"It is simply that I like to see people's faces," Mr. Loeb explained. And he added sadly: "The faces of young people today are closed and secret."

The old painter looked into the faces of the young wherever he found them—at the beach, at the movies, in coffee houses, or on the streets. He would have liked to talk to them, to get to know them, but they shut themselves away from him. It made him feel uncomfortable, as though he didn't belong there, as though he were a visitor in the world. You go along, he thought, in your own time; and then suddenly one day it isn't your time any longer, and the streets are full of strangers. Whom do they take after?

He had one pupil, John Kuzik: this young man worked in a small market in Venice. He had a humble job, nothing like a grocery clerk or a checker; he swept floors and carried out cartons.

For this he was paid a few dollars a week and given the use of a loft over the market as a living place. He had an old bed in it, and his easel, a gas ring, a washbowl; and there was a rusty toilet down the hall. He got enough money each week to buy the paints he needed and a few yards of canvas; he bought his groceries wholesale at the market, and now and then he had enough left over for a meal at a cheap restaurant or a small café.

Kuzik paid Max when he could—a dollar a lesson; or he brought sausages and groceries to the beach for supper, and sometimes wood for the fire. Because he worked during the day, Kuzik painted mostly at night or very early in the morning. He had no friends; his family lived on a farm in Oklahoma. He was often cold and always hungry, but when he was painting he was happy.

"From me," Max said to him when he first came to the garage, "you will only learn to paint things the way they look. Not pretty, necessarily, but recognizable. No three-headed monsters, no holes, no squares, no private conversations. If you want to paint pictures like the new painters, go somewhere else."

"No, sir," Kuzik had said, looking around him at Max's pictures—the heads of Mrs. Bloemendal, a clown, a street in Ocean Park with the sea at the end of it; "this will do fine."

Not that he wanted to imitate Max Loeb. A young painter has to find his own way, but someone has to set him on the road. Then he'll go where he wants to go. Jon Kuzik wasn't interested in history; he didn't want to do portraits. But he wasn't interested in monsters, either, or in holes. He wanted to paint the world he saw around him, in the hard, clear light and the sharp, dark shadows in which he saw it. "Learn to paint the air," Max told him. "Then you'll have your light."

They were sitting on the cold sand of the Playa del Rey in the evening, on an old blanket, looking at the embers of the fire, from which they could still feel a glow of warmth on their faces. "The eye travels through the air," said Max, "and as it travels, it sees. When you fall in love, you will paint from the heart; then you will do faces and figures."

Young Jon Kuzik supposed that Max was right. "I wouldn't know," he said shyly. He had never been in love, and he rarely thought about it. He wondered if Max was in love with his landlady, and if so, what it was like for them. As far as he was concerned, love was for people who wrote books, or had money, or for young people who had nothing else to do. He was in love with light.

Light: to get it down on canvas the way it was; the young, morning light like cold, clear water, the sparkling light between the winter rains, the summer light like an opal, the blue-green mist of evening—firelight, moonlight, sunlight on a wall, on water, even on a face . . . any face; light, that was what he loved.

The old painter talked to his pupil about the past, about his years in Paris, where he had studied at the atelier Julian. "It was where many Americans went to school," he said, "and other foreigners like myself. Julian was not himself a great painter, but he was a great teacher." He told him how he had seen Matisse with his own eyes, and Bracque and Vlaminck and poor, lonely, addled Utrillo and his famous mother, the Valadon. He remembered the Butte, the morning smells of Montmartre and the white dome of Sacre Coeur high above Paris, and the sky of spring, tender and shining, with its gentle clouds low in the south over the Touraine. "In those days," he said, "to be young, in Paris—that was to be really young, and to be happy even when things were sad. Everywhere you heard the young voices, eager and full of hope; it was a new world, even the rebels enjoyed themselves. Everybody was a Columbus. . . . Nobody remembers it the way it was any more, nobody remembers the joy."

He encouraged Jon to talk about his own past, his boyhood on the farm in Oklahoma. "You have something to be grateful for," he told him, "because so much of your childhood was spent in the fresh air. I was born in Europe, in a poor quarter of a small city. We had music, but not much milk, and the weather was not very good. Also, no oranges."

"We didn't have oranges," said Jon; "we ate beans, and pork. There was plenty of milk, though. But fresh air, winter and summer? Mr. Loeb, you don't know Oklahoma. We had mostly snow in winter, and in summer it would get real hot. I never did like the plains for light, not where we were toward the north. What I mostly aim to do someday . . ."

But Max wouldn't let young Kuzik talk about the future. "Listen," he said; "do you know anybody who has a future? Who has a future? the artist? Usually after he is dead. So what kind of future is that? When it is all over, they say hooray for what he did the day before yesterday. Who could be sure, who could say with belief during his lifetime that he had a future? Van Gogh? Modigliani? Rembrandt? Only Picasso."

He thought for a moment. "And Dali," he added.

"Men of such vanity that it becomes important. Of course," he admitted with a sigh, "they also know how to paint."

"I guess you either have luck," said Jon, "or you don't."

"Everybody has luck," said Max Loeb; "more or less. Without any luck at all, I would be dead a thousand times over. Luck is what comes to you when you are not looking, and when you think nothing is coming to you at all."

He nodded his head, like an old owl. "Luck is what comes to you from left field," he said. "Like the sports writers tell you."

CHAPTER 2

THE old man lay quiet in the dark, breathing the smell of the jasmine outside his window. He was having one of his night frights; he was afraid of dying, afraid of the death which was waiting for him someday not too far off, and from which there was no escape. From everything else in the world—from mumps and accidents and even the atom bomb—there was the possibility of avoidance; but not from death. He felt fragile and old; the end might come that very night, for all he knew; he might fall asleep and never wake up again. What if he dreamed? and never woke again to the good light, to the fresh air and the sounds of day . . . but went instead, led by that dream, with only that dream left to him, into the darkness that was so much darker than anything he had ever known. What if it were no friendly dream, but a nightmare, a worry of grief and departure?

He saw himself shut away, alone, in a small, airless box underneath the ground, out of sight and sound, no one to hear him if he cried from loneliness or terror. . . . It was enough to give a man claustrophobia. His heart beat, and a slight perspiration came out on his body. I must think of something else very quickly, he told himself; I will try to remember the happy times, I will think about Vienna, I will remember Florence in the spring, looking down from Fiesole at twilight, with . . . with whom? He had forgotten; it was long ago. A girl, he thought, with brown hair; what was her name? Jo? Josephine? Or was that somewhere else, and at another time?

Whoever it was, he hadn't planned it that way. It was always the same, he thought: the good things came from out there, which was to say from where he didn't expect them. Like the time he had been starving in Munich, and the owner of that gallery—what was it? the Strasser? Streitzer?— had seen one of his paintings in a bake shop where he had left it to pay for a loaf of bread and two pieces of apple cake. Or the time in Paris, at Soutine's studio in Montparnasse—was it Soutine or Kisling?—where he had met the American novelist and had agreed to paint his portrait for the price of a steamship ticket to the States. They had both been drunk, and the next day the American had left for a month in Italy; but when he got back, he sat for his portrait just the same. It was not a bad portrait, as it turned out, and Max had come to America cabin-class. And then there was the year he had been resident artist at that college

—or was it a university?—in the Middle West: Indiana, perhaps, or Illinois; he was always getting them confused. For that matter, his finding Mrs. Bloemendal and her garage . . . Nothing had ever been the way he had planned it.

He had never married. But always, when he was loneliest, some woman . . .

And yet . . .

And yet he was—had always been at heart— timid: what his friend, the great Coby Gilman liked to call a timid little man. He thought of all the wives not married, the lovers not taken, the opportunities missed, out of diffidence, timidity, the desire not to intrude. Vienna, Paris, New York, that place in Illinois—or was it Indiana? Louisa, Christine, Babette, Jacqueline . . . and how many Margarets! The lost hopes, the disasters . . .

The good things, when they came, came from left field, like an express train. But Who was out there?

He didn't know, and he didn't think that anybody else knew, either. It seemed to him that the stars and their systems, the roofless firmament, the earth itself, the virus, the oyster, and the elephant, were forever beyond mortal grasp, beyond human understanding. How could the finite mind probe the infinite? How could man, imprisoned in his three dimensions and traveling through the fourth, describe the fifth, and sixth—or seventh?

Hermione Bloemendal, with whom he had discussed this problem on one occasion, had answered simply: "Through faith."

She was Catholic by birth, and although she did not keep all the Fast Days, or go to Confession very often, when it came to eternity, her mind was made up and serene. "Put your faith up high," she said. "I'd like to," he had answered, "but I can't see God out there among the galaxies."

"What have the galaxies got to do with it?" asked Hermione.

What indeed? thought Max; and gazed at her with fondness and respect. Why do I ask so many questions, he thought, knowing that I would not understand the answers if they were given me?

Maybe if I had crossed the Red Sea with Moses, or stood with Jesus on Calvary, I wouldn't have so much trouble. As it is, I have to accept everything at second hand, which is no good for an artist.

The truth is, he thought, I am afraid to die; and these metaphysical goings-on have nothing to do with it. If I do not get my thoughts on to more practical, everyday matters, I won't sleep all night.

He doubted neither Power nor Spirit; in fact— and this was his weakness—he doubted nothing and accepted everything. In a universe so mysterious, how was it possible to rule anything out? "Why not?" he liked to say; and "Prove to me it is impossible!"

When he was young, with the warm blood and the unrelenting body, the whole wide world was home to him; he felt at home in it where he was; he was no traveler. But that was gone; at ebb tide in his life, things were different. His heart beat more slowly, was less hot; and the world, which had once been so large, seemed to have shrunk until it was hardly any bigger than Santa Monica and Playa del Rey. Even so, he didn't feel at home in it; it was more like being a visitor, on his way—where?

He didn't know. He had loved people and believed in them, long ago; it seemed like long ago, when he was young. He didn't mean love affairs, though he had had his share of those, too, but a simple love of people generally, for the sake of their goodness and their trouble on earth.

He had no illusions about life, which he knew to be painful and often sad. And yet it seemed to him in those days that people had been good and kind at least part of the time. And love had had a glow, a tenderness, a shyness, an ardor, even—well, no one was ashamed of it, at any rate. It was something, it gave people joy, it gave them sorrow, it brought them to their knees in worship—not of God necessarily, but of something.

A man knew where he was then, and where he was going. Hope was his road, and love his destination. Max Loeb had known where he was. Now he was like a traveler going down a hill at twilight, without a home. It was so long since he had seen anyone look at him with love.

Work: that was the thing. When he was working he felt alive and often young again. It wasn't always easy; sometimes in the middle of a picture he'd lay down his brushes and think: I've done all this before, why do it over again? Work had to be a progress to be a comfort to a man; merely to repeat what he'd done before was to go through a tired journey without surprises or delights.

To work and to love—that was all a man needed to keep the night frights away. When his thoughts were about life, there wasn't room in them for death. He was too old for love; with what? a granddaughter? He left that to more audacious men.

He began to plan a picture in his mind; he would get a professional model to pose for him. A full figure against a blue curtain, with a bowl of—what? Flowers? No—a bowl of cooked shellfish, the tomato reds against the blue . . .

He had a moment of eagerness, of enthusiasm,

even; but then it left him, and he sighed dispiritedly. He had painted that same picture at St.
Tropez on the Côte d'Azur; and he had sold it,
too, to some little dealer in Toulon, for three hundred francs. Matisse himself was in the south of
France that year. The franc was down to 3.7 cents,
and he had got about ten dollars for it. Not bad; it
was more than Modigliani got for some of his. Until Modigliani was dead, of course, and then his
canvases were worth a fortune.

He was no Modigliani, and his pictures would
never be worth any more than they were now. He
hadn't invented a new style, he hadn't broken any
new ground, he had painted only what he saw,
and what anyone could see. For people like myself, he thought, there is no appeal to posterity;
we please the senses only of our own generation.
The newly opened eyes do not see us, the young,
unwaxed ears do not hear us, they are tuned to
new sights and new sounds. And those whom we
please die off year after year.

At least, he thought gently, we must believe

that these new sights and sounds delight them, even though to us they are without harmony or form, without dignity, and without any human characteristics whatever.

In her room in the main house, Hermione Bloemendal also sighed, and stirred restlessly in her bed. She kept her windows closed at night, the smell of jasmine did not trouble her. She, too, lay awake, and wondered whether to make pancakes for breakfast and take some over to Mr. Loeb in the garage. Perhaps someday he would notice something about her besides her face.

They kept their windows closed at night in France, too; he had told her that. It was something about the night air . . . How could a face have history in it? History was battles and wars and presidential elections. . . .

She tried to remember if there was sour milk in the icebox for the pancakes. They were better with sour milk.

And dates, of course: eighteen hundred and something, nineteen hundred and something . . .

She wrinkled her nose in the darkness, she was never good at dates. Year after year, and the years went by . . . It was discouraging. Who cared when Columbus discovered America? Things had changed since then.

Jon Kuzik slept under his worn blanket on his lumpy mattress in his room over the market. In his dreams he was not a painter, but he had no regrets. He was on the farm, going out with a pail in the dark early morning to get milk from the cows. He had had the dream before; in his dream, there was never any milk, and it made him sad and ashamed. But always, when he woke, he forgot about it.

And under an overhang in the cliff north of the Playa del Rey, Halys Smith, twenty, of Oregon City, lay huddled under her thin raincoat, hungry and cold, waiting for the morning to come; sleeping a little, and waking, and sleeping again, and dreaming only of warmth.

C H A P T E R 3

Two nights later Halys Smith fell on the sand in front of Max Loeb's fire. In the meanwhile she had had one bowl of soup and a plate of spaghetti given her by the owner of a small café, several cups of coffee at a soda fountain, and a bottle of orange pop. She had spent two days at the amusement pier at Ocean Park looking for work; she had washed dishes, she would have been glad to have taken the job regularly, but she was only offered enough for the soup and the spaghetti. "Come back day after tomorrow," said the owner of the café; "tonight is my regular washer."

She was too thin and wan to be of interest to any of the photographic studios in the vicinity, although she thought of herself as a model, or had once, when she was younger, in Oregon. She had been searching in the refuse cans for something left over from the early suppers, and, weaving her way lightheadedly across the sand, had stumbled in front of the fire at which Max and Jon Kuzik were heating an iron kettle full of soup. Once she had fallen, she just lay there and cried a little.

Max went over to her, and when he felt how cold her hands were, he got her to sit up and drew her closer to the fire. "Thank you," she said; "I don't know why . . ." and lay down again on the sand and closed her eyes.

"I think she's sick," said Jon.

Max Loeb shook his head. "She's hungry," he said simply.

Jon looked down at the prostrate girl with surprise. She was thin, all right; and she was shivering. Maybe she was hungry; he'd often been hungry, and cold, too, but he'd never cried about it. She must be pretty delicate, he thought: highstrung.

"It can't be that bad," he said. He meant it to sound comforting; it wasn't his fault that it sounded unfeeling; it was just embarrassment.

Halys sat up slowly; she was weary and sick, and when she thought of the refuse cans, it was like drowning in a wave of shame. She hated herself, and she hated this boy, this young man . . . whatever he was. "Why can't it?" she said. "What would you know about it?" Her voice was light, it was like a thread of sound, it seemed to have no breath behind it. Her great dark eyes in her white face turned to Max. "You got anything to eat?" she demanded.

They both were silent while she gulped down a

bowl of the hot soup. Max looked away out of kindness, but Jon stared at her without liking, as though she were some strange sort of animal. "Here," he said at last, awkwardly, holding out his own piece of bread to her: "take it. I've had plenty."

She didn't thank him, but she took the bread and bit into it hungrily. She doesn't like me, he thought; he was sorry he'd given her the bread. What do I owe her? he asked himself. Nothing.

Because she was still shivering, Max put his coat around her, and she hugged herself inside it with her thin arms. But as she began to feel better, she grew shy, and didn't know what to say. "I guess that was pretty corny," she said at last; "falling down like that. I could have burned myself." She gave a light, self-conscious laugh. "I guess I was hungry," she said.

Jon didn't know what to say, or what to do. He kicked at the sand, and looked away, up and down the beach. "Well," he said at last, "I guess you were hungry, all right."

And he glanced at Max, to see if he had said the proper thing. But Max was looking at Halys. "How did it happen?" Max asked her. "Do you live here?"

Again the light laugh, as though it were a shield to hide behind. "Sure," she said. "I live up the beach a ways. On a pile of sand."

"I see," said Max gently; and Halys put her head down on her arms and wept.

"Excuse me," said Jon. "I've got to go to the gent's."

The way she cried, so quietly and so bitterly; he didn't like to watch it. It made him ashamed for her, and ashamed for himself, too, for not doing anything about it. He got up and walked away across the sand toward the sea. Beyond the last row of fires it was dark; suddenly there were stars overhead above the water, and the waves were rumbling in and breaking on the shore in a gray smother. To the south he could see the red and white chimney of the Hyperion, and farther still the Edison Company towers, and beyond them in the blue night air the deeper loom of Palos Verdes, like a shadow in the sky, picked out with silver pinpoints of light. A plane went over, swimming above him like the belly of a fish, and in the north the lights of Malibu shone small and low across the night-dark water.

It was queer how sad he felt: sad, and angry, too, for some reason or other—but why? and at whom? It wasn't the girl's fault she was hungry. She's thin as a bone, he thought; she doesn't look like she'd last the week out.

He didn't know why he should feel so bitter about it. Heck, he told himself, it's got nothing to do with me. But the feeling of sadness wouldn't leave him; though actually it was more a kind of loneliness.

He tramped on over the wet beach with long strides, his feet dragging a little in the sand. The cold waves coming in ran runnels of foam around his feet; already the fires of the Playa in their concrete circles were behind him, and the full night was around him. There was no moon; it was ghostly down by the water, with the beach stretching away ahead of him, dim and dimmer and gone, and the gray sea tumbling beside him, rising unseen out there in the darkness, and then falling with a roar to race up the sand at him.

He kept seeing the girl's white, scornful face, the way she looked at him, half defiant, half pitiful. . . . She had been looking in the refuse cans; she must have been half out of her mind to do a thing like that. A young girl, he thought; she's no older than me, and she hasn't got anybody.

That people could be so lonely in the world was a profound shock to the young man's nature. He'd never really thought about people before; he just hadn't had cause, he would have said, to notice them. Except as bodies, that is, the way he'd notice horses or cows in a field as he was passing through, but not in the way of consideration, of wondering about their lives or what was going on. There were a lot of people in the world, but mostly they didn't speak to each other, and he'd never given it much thought.

But when they did, it was like shattering a silence. It was pitiful, that was what it was: pitiful. Suddenly it made his heart ache.

He felt bitter about it, too; he didn't want people to be pitiful. It frightened him; he wanted people to be hard, and not to be squashed like beetles. What was the good of being a man if he could be squashed as easily as a grasshopper?

He remembered his sisters crying now and then on the farm in Oklahoma, but that was from rage, or from a crack on the shins, or fear, or the colic; it wasn't cold and quiet, like this girl's, and lonely, as if there wasn't any help for anything or any hope for anything. . . .

There wasn't anything he could do, anyway.

He walked a long way up the beach before he turned to retrace his steps, facing the far-off little pools of fire again. He half expected—and more than half hoped—to find the girl gone when he got back, but she was still there, wrapped in Max's old coat. She had been talking, apparently; but when he appeared out of the shadowy distance with the darkness of the sea behind him, she stopped suddenly and looked up at him in fright, and at the same time defiantly and with a sort of pleading.

He sat down and drew his knees up to his chin. "I went for a walk along the beach," he said.

Max looked at him curiously. He knew that Jon was upset about something, but he didn't know what. With sudden, rueful insight, he thought: he dislikes this girl!

"Miss Smith is from Oregon," he said, as though that explained everything. "She has been telling me about herself."

Jon gave a grunt; it was an altogether noncommittal sound. But he angled a quick glance at Halys before he turned back to the fire. Oregon, he thought. It made him feel better. She didn't belong there on the beach, she was from up north, it wasn't his problem.

So that's what a girl from Oregon looks like, he thought.

But Max was seeing in his mind the rocky coast and the dark, frosted mountains, the green, icy rivers and the pines, and smelling the rain and the sun-scattered, cloud-shadowed air over the forests and the farms. . . .

"We are taking Miss Smith home with us," he said.

CHAPTER 4

"In the garage, the two of you?" said Mrs. Bloemendal doubtfully. "Well, now, there's a thing!"

Halys said nothing; she looked humble and hungry, and she didn't want to make any trouble. But Max was indignant. "Who said a garage?" he asked. "A man's home is his home."

"It's not that I've got a thing against you," Hermione said to Halys, "or that I wouldn't trust the two of you to behave. But it hasn't got what I'd call accommodations for a young lady."

A young lady, thought Halys helplessly; no one had ever called her that, as far as she could remember. "What do you do, dear?" asked Hermione. "What work are you in?"

Halys hesitated a moment. "I'm an actress," she said at last. Well, why not? It made as much sense as anything else. Everybody in high school said she could be as good as Julie Harris if she'd only stick to it; and so did Mr. Pfeifer, the dramatic coach. But how did a girl stick to it, in Oregon City, with a mother who drank too much, and a grandmother who worked in a beauty salon in Eugene; not really a grandmother, either, but just the third wife of her grandfather; and an uncle heaven only knew where, and nobody else?

"I've been on my own," she said, "since I was fourteen."

"So, you belong to the profession," said Hermione, with a pleased look. A moment later she asked in surprise: "At fourteen?"

Halys shrugged her shoulders. As a matter of fact, she'd been a lot of things—a baby-sitter, a waitress, a carhop, an apple-picker; she'd even done commercials for a local television studio in Portland, modeling cheap furs and pointing out the advantages of gas ovens and stoves. "I've been on television," she said, "and things like that."

She might have been a dancer if she'd ever had the right kind of lessons. She saw herself the year she'd gone to dancing school, the year her mother had a job with the telephone company, and they had a little money—a skinny, dark-haired little kid, with a runny nose. Everybody said she had talent.

"I was a dancer myself," said Hermione.

Halys flushed and looked away. "I guess you wouldn't call it acting, what I did," she said. "Selling stoves, and things like that."

She has no figure, thought Hermione: nothing

. . . or so little of it . . . She'd never do for a model. Like Mr. Loeb said, without a head she wouldn't scarcely give out any information at all. Hermione relaxed. "It's a hard life," she said: "selling anything."

"For tonight," said Max, "Miss Smith will sleep on the sofa in my studio."

It isn't my affair, thought Hermione; the girl is of age. There was, after all, no sin in sleeping on a sofa, even in a garage. Mr. Loeb could call it a studio, but it was a garage.

"I can let you have an extra blanket," she said to Max; "you better come along and get it."

Alone in the studio with Halys, Jon stood first on one foot and then on the other. He couldn't think of anything to say; he had a feeling that things were happening too fast. A few hours ago they hadn't even known this girl. . . .

She had her back to him; after a while she said in a muffled voice over her shoulder: "What are you staring at?"

"I wasn't staring," he said. "I was only thinking."

"What?" she demanded. "Thinking about what?"

He gave a helpless gesture. "I don't know," he said. "It was like . . . you staying here with the old man. . . ."

"You think that's bad, or something?"

"No," he said. "I didn't mean anything bad. What I meant was—it'll be different for him, having somebody around."

The girl's thin body stiffened, and then all at once she seemed to droop. "You mean I'll be in the way," she said. She sounded small, and close to tears.

Oh, no, he thought; not again!

"I didn't mean you'd be in the way," he said. "I only meant it was different. I don't know what I meant."

"Yes," she said. "I guess it's different, all right. For me, too."

But a few seconds later she whirled on him in a kind of fury. "What else can I do?" she cried. "Tell me that!"

Jon backed away, his hands flung up in front of

him as though to ward her off. "Take it easy," he said; "take it easy! Nobody says you got to do anything."

They were staring at each other like two fierce birds from opposite ends of the room when Max came back. He brought, in addition to the blanket, a pair of cotton pajamas belonging to Mrs. Bloemendal. "You'd better go home," he said to Jon. "This young woman needs to get to bed."

"Well, good night," Jon said, and went out and closed the door behind him.

Halys undressed behind the old screen that Max used for his models, while he made up the sofa into something resembling a bed. "It's no first-class hotel accommodation," he told her, "but it's softer than a beach." "It'll probably seem like heaven," said Halys.

She came out from behind the screen dressed in Hermione's pajamas; they made her look even smaller and more lost than before. She had rolled up the sleeves and the bottoms, but they were still too big for her. "I guess I look pretty funny," she said, looking down at herself. "Like a clown or something."

"A clown is never funny," said Max; "he is only sad. Why we laugh is because he is so small in such a big world. It is like a mouse conducting a symphony: such efforts, but the man with the big horn cannot see him. I will get you some hot milk. It will make you sleep better."

Halys turned to face him. "Is that what you want?" she asked. "For me to sleep?"

The old painter looked at her in surprise. "Of course," he said gently.

She looked away, and went over and sat on the edge of the couch. "I may throw up the milk," she said, "the way I feel."

"You'll feel better in the morning," said Max.

"I thought . . ." she said. "I didn't know . . ."

"Go to sleep," said Max. "Say your prayers."

She lay down on the sofa with her face to the wall, while Max heated a pan of milk on the gas ring that served him as a stove. He took it over to her, and she drank it without saying anything.

Then she turned back to the wall again and pulled the blanket up over her head. Max took the cup and the pan to the washbasin, and cleaned up, washed his face and hands, brushed his teeth, and behind the screen slipped awkwardly into his old-fashioned flannel nightgown. Then he put out the light and climbed into his own bed, which creaked with his weight. "Good night," he said, but Halys didn't answer.

Outside, the moonlight lay still and pale on the patio, and pale and green on the flowering bushes. The summer smell of jasmine stole in at the window; and, looking up, Max could see the night-blue sky through the dusty panes of the skylight over his head. A mockingbird trilled in a tree down the street in the lonely air.

He lay still in his bed, feeling warm and light and happy. There is someone here, he thought; another soul, I am not alone. If I cried out, it would be noticed. He had been alone a long time, he had forgotten what it was like to have someone in the room with him, in the darkness . . . a woman, a girl, small and lost, a daughter, a granddaughter, able to keep the night frights away. Probably, he thought, that is how people came to live together in the first place, to have company in the black nights in the caves around the smoky fires; otherwise they would have been too afraid of one another. Although, he thought wryly, at his age in those days a man would already have been bones for the hyena. Love and fear, he thought: what else is man's story? Sometimes love has led the world, and sometimes fear; and lately fear, and love is nowhere.

You have only to look at what the painters are doing, he said, although no one was listening to him, to see that love is out of date. He spoke only in his own mind; he addressed himself to an audience which didn't exist. Can you love people, he asked, with two heads or three eyes? or who look like something painted by children on a fence? These are not paintings done out of love for the human race. And the young people, who in my time were living and writing their love stories—

what are they doing? Who knows? We hear from them only when they are in trouble with the police.

Tomorrow, he thought inconsequentially, I will see that she gets a hot bath. I should have thought of it sooner, but I didn't.

The moon went down in the west, and in the middle of the night, in the darkness, he woke, hearing a light, thin sound like a child crying. Oh, now, he thought unhappily, what is it? and called out to her in a low voice: "Miss Smith?" But there was no answer, only a sigh, and a small hiccup. He would have liked to comfort her, but he didn't know how. It'll be better in the morning, he thought, when she's had breakfast; leave her be with her grief, she has a right to it. The girl was quiet again, and after a while he fell asleep again, not knowing what else to do.

Hermione Bloemendal had no reason to stay awake; she slept and dreamed. She dreamed of the Venus de Milo: "Down the long hall she glistens like a star. . . ." She remembered reading that long ago, it was a poem, and by a woman with the name of Lazarus. Strange how things came back to her from her school days; but she could never tell when. That was the name, Lazarus, a Jewish name like him that was brought to life and risen by Our Lord. There was no one had a figure like the Irish. Take her husband, Mr. Bloemendal; as kind a man as you'd want to meet, but there was more around the middle of him than across the shoulders. . . . The thing was, in her dream she'd had the figure: she had the arms, but no head. Never having seen the statue herself, except in a school book, there didn't seem to be anything out-of-the-way about it. Her head had never been remarkable.

And what a poor, thin thing the girl was, though she'd likely fill out when she had some food in her. And the old man taking her in with him, the way he did. Not that he was so old, at that, when you came right down to it, and no ordinary man, either, him being a painter and having knowledge in his own profession.

She went back to sleep again with a look of appreciation on her face.

But, in his room above the market, Jon lay awake and stared into the blackness. He couldn't get over it, all so fast, and there she was in with old Max, and the two of them sleeping in the same room within a crawl of each other. It wasn't any of his business, it was nothing to him, but he couldn't get over it.

For the first time he thought of Max as a man, and he had to think of him as an old man; and the great stretch of years, the difference in their ages, lay there like a desert between them. He had to think of him as a man who could have a woman to stay with him; and that was something he'd never . . . well, he couldn't get over it. But that's the way Max was, after all; it was hard to imagine it, an old man like that from whom the heat must have departed long ago. Or maybe not; how did he know? There was a sadness about it; he knew he'd never be like that himself in his sixties. When he was old he'd be old, and satisfied, and young women could sleep in their raincoats in the middle of the Mojave Desert for all he'd care.

It was the girl's fault; she'd come up to them and asked for it. So now she had it . . . turning things upside-down . . . He guessed he'd never forget her voice when she asked him what he was staring at. He'd never forget the dislike in it.

But she had cried, and he thought of the way she'd turned on him and asked him what else could she do. He hadn't made much of an answer, and that was the truth. He perspired a little in his bed; he felt uncomfortable, and unhappy. Maybe he'd ask at the market in the morning; they might have something. Best not be too hopeful about it; they wouldn't be likely to use a girl in the storeroom.

Look, he said to himself for the tenth time, it's none of your business.

She was there, asleep in Max's room, in those old pajamas of Mrs. Bloemendal's, her little slender bones thrusting out of the rolled-up sleeves, her great dark eyes closed. He remembered the smell of jasmine on his way home, and another smell of honeysuckle, and the cold sweet air and the lemon-pale moonlight on the walls and the houses. . . .

Lemon-pale—that was it. He stared into the dark, trying to see the moonlight, trying to see the pale colors in the air. Tomorrow he'd try to get it down on canvas; he mustn't forget it—lemon-pale.

When Max awoke, the sun was just rising, the light outside his studio yellow-gray with a flush of pink in it, and the bushes gray-green and dark. Halys was sitting at the window, looking out at the new day; all he could see was the back of her head. The thin, light-boned body was still, unmoving; whatever she was thinking, he had no way of knowing.

But she was there. Max sighed and smiled and closed his eyes and opened them again. It was like the old days, it was a good waking-up.

CHAPTER 5

Max fixed breakfast for them both—coffee, eggs, and bacon. They ate together on the battered old table where Max kept his brushes and his paints; seated in front of the window with the paint-smeared table top between them, they looked out at the patio where the early sun lay white and gleaming on the stone and made black shadows in the earth along the borders.

Halys was shy; she kept her eyes down, and smiled in a timid, beseeching way. Max, on the other hand, looked around his room with a feeling of enjoyment. He was reminded of other mornings and other years; it wasn't the first time a woman had been there in his studio when he woke up. In Europe, when he was younger, it was something to be expected: an artist was only alone as much as he wanted to be, unless he was unlucky, or very poor, or in love, or for some other reason. And always, or almost always, the little strangeness at first, strangers getting used to each other; even in love, the strangeness at first. But there was never anything one-sided about it; a model in those days gave her services or herself with equal pride, like a wife or a business woman. There was always a dignity about it. Not, of course, the ladies of the evening, the cocottes, the women of the streets; they weren't models at all, and neither were the book heroines, the nymphs at the bars, the golden girls of the novelists. He had never known any golden girls, his models were all, simply and wholly, models.

Sometimes they were good cooks, too.

Halys glanced up at him from under her lashes. She saw him in his faded dressing gown, tattered at the cuffs, tied round his middle with string, and smiling a little, thinking of something. "Did you sleep all right?" she asked timidly. "I was so ashamed."

Max looked at her in alarm. "Please," he said; "why should you be ashamed? You were frightened. And very cold. So you got warm, that is all."

A little more color came into her cheeks, and she looked down and away. She nodded her head. "Yes," she said. "I didn't mean . . . I only meant . . . I was afraid maybe I'd bothered you."

He was smiling at her across the table. "There was no bother," he said. "It was a comfort to me. I fell asleep very soon." He leaned toward her earnestly. "Believe me," he said; "it was a comfort."

She didn't answer, stirring her coffee and looking down into the cup.

"I am afraid at night sometimes," he said.

"I know," she said in a low voice; but he shook a finger at her. "You shouldn't know," he said. "When I was your age I didn't know either."

"Maybe we grow faster nowadays," she said.

"So you grow faster," he agreed. But he thought to himself: you are in such a hurry, you young people. And in a hurry for what? To achieve something in the world? No—to enjoy everything all at once. What is the good of hurrying so fast? Everything will be over before you know it, and then what? One thinks of his own generation as being immortal and endless, until he begins to count the friends who have died.

After breakfast, Max arranged with Mrs. Bloemendal for Halys's hot bath, and then went out into the patio and sat down in the sun to read the morning newspaper. As usual, it was full of trouble: assaults, local scandals, threats from union leaders, boasts and alarms by the military, traffic smash-ups, a wholesale killing by a lunatic released from an asylum, demands for more taxes, angry notes from Russia—a history of the times. There was also one installment of a series of articles concerned with the treatment of arthritis through oiling the joints of the body. However, looking for the book review, Max found it in a small box at the bottom of the page; clearly, said Max to himself, the owner-publisher of this great newspaper does not believe in books, but he believes in oil.

And, sighing, he threw back his head and looked for a moment into the sun, to strengthen his eyes. "Oh, my country!" he exclaimed: "what have I adopted?"

Presently he went inside, and stretched and prepared a small canvas. I will just sketch the head, he thought, as she comes from her bath, and with a towel wrapped around her hair like a turban.

"Not to sell," he told her; "only to teach myself, a study, for something I have in mind."

She seated herself obediently in a chair in front

of the screen, and took the pose he wanted, her head a little to one side, looking straight before her. After a while the quiet settled into her, and she dreamed—of nothing in particular; of happiness, perhaps, of a life without trouble. What does a girl dream of? Love: but love comes without a face at such times, it is a tranquility, a warmth of heart, a season in the sun. Her eyes glazed, her mouth opened slightly, and she gave a small snore.

It made no difference to Max; at that moment what interested him was the bone structure. When her head fell forward, he waited until she lifted it again with a look of embarrassment. But after a second fall he realized that she was still too lost and too weary, and laid down his charcoal. "It is not easy to pose," he said; "sit out in the sun for a while, and rest."

She fell asleep in the patio, and Hermione from her window upstairs gazed down at her. Well, she's a poor thing at that, thought Hermione, and worn out; and if there's a love affair there, you can have my right leg. But there'll be more sheets and towels for the laundry, and I wonder does Mr. Loeb know it.

He did not. At noon he awakened Halys, and sent her to the market to get something for them both for lunch. "For myself, at lunch," he explained, "I can do with a cracker and a bit of cheese, or even with nothing if I am painting; but you need something hot, like a good soup from a can, with noodles." He went to the old tobacco jar where he kept his money, and took out a crumpled dollar bill. "Get what you like," he said, "but avocados are cheap now and nice and filling."

The market was not very far; Halys walked down the street, past the little sunny stucco houses, feeling curiously lightheaded and almost lighthearted. It was almost like being disembodied, and suddenly without a care. Off to one side, down a side street, she could see the sea shining in the sun; it no longer seemed to have anything to do with her. The people she passed had friendly, human faces, the houses had windows through which one could look. . . . Nothing surprised her. She wasn't even surprised to find Jon at the market, with a soiled and somewhat tattered apron over his corduroy shirt and his Levi's. "Hi," he said without friendliness.

They looked at each other indifferently, coldly, like strangers; withdrawn, but with an awareness of each other, a sense of something, some fright or hunger, an event shared, something between them whether for good or ill. He helped her pick out the few things she wanted. "You'd better take the noodle soup," he said, replacing a can of green pea, "because Mr. Loeb likes it." He knew more about his teacher's likes and dislikes than she did, and he was glad to tell her so.

When she was finished, he carried the bag out to the street for her. "I'm not supposed to go any further," he said.

"That's all right," she said, and took the bag and started back to the studio. She no longer felt lighthearted or disembodied; people's faces had lost their friendliness. The bag was heavy; she felt like crying again.

Jon stood looking after her for a moment; and then he turned and went back into the market. He was disturbed; and, without quite knowing why, disappointed; except that seeing her again wasn't the way he'd expected. He was vexed with her, and with himself; she could have been a little more friendly, he thought, considering. Or he could at least have told her how he'd tried to get her a job—something, anything—at the market, and how he'd been turned down. Instead, she hadn't said anything to him, or he to her, except about the soup. It was clear that she didn't like him any better than he liked her, and that they'd never get along. Each came between the other and Max like the shadow on the moon. The moon— that reminded him; what was it he'd wanted to remember? Lemon-yellow; was that it? Lemon-yellow? It certainly didn't sound right; not for the moon.

A girl like that could move in on a man like Max, an old man who didn't know any better, and make a fool of him. The first thing, she'd be living there as though she owned the place.

Not that she looked mean, or anything like that; she wasn't bad-looking, really, not pretty, but with nice enough looks, of a kind. There was something about her face that made him think about the bones under it. Bones would be white once they were out from under the skin, ivory, veined, and speckled; like old shells washed up by the sea. Bones were people, really; or people were bones. Like a land was the granite under it. You farmed the topsoil and got wheat and cucumbers, but the water came from the rock. A man could paint the bones under a face if he knew how, the way van Gogh could paint the land: the solid land, the water under the loam, and the air above.

Max did no work that afternoon; he let Halys keep house for him instead, by borrowing a broom from Mrs. Bloemendal and sweeping in the corners. It was the labor of a child rather than a woman; she made sudden dabs with the broom, or slow, vague sweeps, working away contentedly, without the numbing realization of what a really clean house ought to look like, never having seen one. Mrs. Bloemendal dropped in on them; she brought a pail and a scrubbing brush, and stood in the doorway looking on in a friendly way; but when she left after a few minutes she took the brush and the pail away with her. "It's very nice, dearie," she said to Halys; "I'm sure Mr. Loeb appreciates what you're doing. I could have got a cleaning woman for you," she said to Max as she went out, "if I'd have known you wanted one."

Halys leaned on her broom and pushed a straggle of hair from off her forehead. "Anyway," she said hopefully, "it's a little better."

"For it to be better is not important," said Max. "The important thing is, how do you feel?"

"Oh, I'm better, too," she said. "I feel all right."

"Well," he said, "that's good." He smiled at her, but she could see that he didn't know what to say next. There was the question of what was to become of her, and it hadn't been decided yet.

She looked at him gravely. Better get it settled, she thought, one way or the other. "Am I going to stay?" she asked.

He stared out of the window for a moment without answering; then he turned back to her where she stood leaning on the broom. "Have you somewhere else to go?" he asked gently.

She shook her head. "No," she said, "but it doesn't matter."

"Stay, then," he said.

After that they both stopped talking for a while. Some decision had been reached, some bridge had been crossed; but what happened next? They thought of the way she had slept in Max's bed—cold, despairing, and innocent—and it made them self-conscious. They wanted to reassure each other, in some way comfort each other.

"This is really a very nice room," she said. "It's cool, too, with the skylight. . . ."

"It faces north. . . ."

"I should think you'd want the sunlight. . . ."

"For a painter, no. . . ."

What comfort was that? They were being polite, like visitors. It would be much better not to say anything at all, simply to smile. They were not unhappy; they were at arm's length, but they could come closer when they wanted to.

Halys broke the silence at last. "Would you like me to go out and get something for supper?" she asked timidly; "like I did at lunch?"

"It is already in the house," said Max. At that moment he decided to cook the supper himself. "I am an old hand," he explained, "on a gas ring. Anyone can open a can; it is what you mix with it that counts." He got up and went to the cupboard in what he called his kitchen; he expanded, he bustled, he made gestures because he was happy and because he had something to do for someone; he was showing off in front of her. "The right herbs," he said: "salt, pepper, butter . . . butter is very important; maybe an egg, slices of onion, another can of something else . . . it is all in the mixing. If you like, I will give you a lesson; come and stand by me and watch how I do it."

"I'd rather sit here where I am," she said. "I'm still sort of tired. I'll sleep tonight, I think."

For the first time she seemed to feel at home; it was her first small speech of acceptance. It sounded flat, and weary; he could feel the little glow inside die down, but it didn't go out altogether. It was still there, it was still enough like the old times.

CHAPTER 6

THE days that followed were happy enough for Max Loeb the painter. But for Jon Kuzik they were days of confusion, empty and baffling. There were three, now, instead of the two there used to be—himself and Max; or were there three at all— and not two, Max and the girl, and Jon left out? Whatever way it was, that close thing they'd had was gone: where they could sit for an hour without talking, or where, if there was any talk, it was easy and natural. Now when he saw Max he didn't know what to say; and the silences, instead of being comfortable were uneasy and embarrassed. He wanted to ask Max what it was like for him to have Halys there; he wanted to ask him if he and Halys were in love, though he couldn't believe it or imagine it. . . . He wanted to ask him: What has happened? Why are we strangers to each other? But he couldn't; and Max volunteered nothing.

So, after two visits to the studio in the evening after work, Jon stayed away. He wasn't happy, and he was lonely. Now, of an evening, he walked along the ocean front by himself, or up and down the streets, looking in the shop windows. It was idle drifting; he didn't feel like painting, and that was the truth. He didn't know if he hated Halys or not; he guessed he probably disliked her as much as anyone. He wished he didn't have to think about her.

But he did think about her; and sometimes when

he climbed the steps to his little room at night, and lay down in the dark, he found himself trembling with some sort of fury or misery or both.

Of all this, Max was innocent and unaware. All he knew was that he was no longer alone, and that he no longer lay awake nights and thought about death. Even in the dark, and at the other end of the room, there was comfort in the girl's company; if he called, she would hear him. And each day she seemed to bloom a little, to feel more at home with him; who knew how it would end? He liked to watch her bustling about in the morning, making the bed and the sofa, washing the dishes; he liked to cook for her and watch her eat, she enjoyed it so much. And on top of it all, she was an excellent model, and he had already made some charcoal studies of her head and her hands; "Like Michelangelo," he said; "the hands are important." They were good hands, still thin, but strong, and sunburned. "A woman's hands," he told her, "they express everything: sadness, love, resignation . . . woman's life and woman's work. . . ."

She held them up in front of her, and looked at them ruefully. "They don't look like they did anything," she said.

"They pose," said Max. "I am thinking of something for them to do." He was already planning, sketching out in his mind his canvas, his picture *On the Beach.*

He had her sit with her head bowed and her arms over her knees, her hands hanging limply. He wanted to get the long clean line of the back under the dress she wore. "Tired," he said, "and a little dreamy, after the day's work."

"Max," she said after a while, not looking up; "I ought to get a job."

"A job?" he said lightly. "You have a job. It's only that I can't afford to pay you."

"It isn't that," she said gravely. "You more than pay me. It's only . . . well, it's living here like this, I mean. I ought to look for work."

"There is nothing easy about finding a job," said Max, "particularly in summer when all the schools and colleges are out, and everybody is looking."

"I could try, anyway."

"Even so," he said slowly, sketching very carefully, paying great attention to the line, "why not live here, at least? To save rent?"

"Because," she said. A moment later she added with an attempt at bravado: "I think your landlady is beginning to worry."

"Well," he said; "so. And you; do you worry?"

"No," she said. "Not . . . exactly."

"What does that mean?"

"I don't want to make trouble for you with Mrs. Bloemendal," she said.

"A man's home is his home," said Max. "Besides —she's a Catholic."

She looked up at him in surprise. "But that's just it," she said.

Max described a long, clean curve with his charcoal. "Don't make any mistake about the Catholics," he said. "They must be the least anxious people in the world. They have heaven waiting for them; so they can afford to overlook a few things here and there. Not in the letter, of course, but in the spirit . . ."

"Well," said Halys doubtfully, "I don't know. The things I've heard . . ."

"Naturally," said Max, "it wasn't always like that. During the Middle Ages, for instance, and as late even as the sixteenth century, the Church burned as many heretics as it could lay its hands on. On the other side, for the two centuries after that, and also at Belsen and Buchenwald, it was the Protestants who burned people."

He squinted at Halys, measuring her with his thumb. "I am amused often," he said, "because the Pope looks so much like one of the Borgias. He is really a very nice fellow, mellow, agreeable, and full of good sense. He would recognize innocence when he saw it.

"So sit with your head a little lower, please, and the arms . . . loosely . . . so. Very nice."

"Just the same," she said after a while, "I think I ought to look for something to do."

With an angry gesture he threw the charcoal to the floor. "Enough is enough!" he cried.

"Are you so tired of it here?"

She was startled; she looked at him with wide eyes, and put the back of her hand to her mouth. "No," she said; "oh, no. Only . . ."

"Then stop the foolishness!" he exclaimed.

He was silent for a moment, bending to pick up the charcoal, which had broken in two. "Come," he said presently; "I will buy you an ice-cream soda."

Sitting at the counter of the drugstore at Hill and Main, Max drank his coffee, and watched Halys with her soda. She still seemed troubled, and kept her eyes on her glass or on the straw from which she was drinking. Presently she made a little, embarrassed movement with her arms, close to her sides. "I didn't realize you were a Catholic," she said. "I'm sorry."

"But I am not!" Max said.

"No?" she exclaimed in surprise. "But I thought . . ."

"Because I am perhaps a little jealous of Catholics?" he asked. "One does not have to be a Catholic to long for a chance at the Catholic heaven. As a matter of fact, my mother was a Catholic; at least, she was born one. My father was an anarchist. I am nothing: a man to whom God only speaks in riddles."

"Yes," said Halys. "It doesn't make much sense, does it?"

Max agreed that it didn't make much sense. "And yet," he declared, "I believe in God. I have faith of a sort: all this couldn't have been an accident."

"All this?" asked Halys, looking at her empty glass with the straw in it. "All what?"

"This little earth," said Max, "and the moving things on it. Oceans and rivers, clouds and tides, men, flowers . . . the spider and the fly, the tiny midge to whom a flea is as big as an elephant . . . the stars blazing and wheeling in their pride, the planets and their moons, too far away to be seen . . . All this is no accident."

"I have no faith at all," said Halys simply.

"And there is also something in man," said Max, "more mysterious even than the flight of birds or a promenade of ants."

She sat there, hunched over the counter, staring off into space. "Things happen in a strange way sometimes," she said. "They really do."

She was thinking—how could she help herself?—of those nights on the beach under the cliff, fishing for scraps in the trash cans. They could have led to the police station, or a home for fallen girls, or, for all she knew, to a work camp . . . Instead they had led to this, a place to live, a soda at the drugstore . . .

"You and Jon," she said.

Jon . . . Where was he keeping himself? And why hadn't he been around?

"Didn't he use to study with you?" she asked.

"He was my whole school," said Max.

Was? He realized suddenly that it had been days since he'd seen him, that Jon no longer came for lessons. Could he have left? gone somewhere without saying good-by? It wasn't like him . . .

"Perhaps he's been sick," he said. "Maybe we ought to inquire."

"I've seen him once or twice at the market," said Halys carelessly. She didn't add that each time he'd been too busy to talk to her. She had a feeling that he didn't want to see her, that he didn't feel friendly toward her. She was used to that from people, even when she couldn't see any reason for it.

"I never learned about religion," she said. "I said a prayer when I was little: 'Now I lay me down to sleep.' It was just something you said before you went to sleep."

" 'I pray the Lord my soul to keep,' " said Max. "It is the best prayer for little children who believe that God is watching over them."

"Nobody watched over me," said Halys. She hesitated, playing with the straw in her glass. "Not till now," she said, and looked up at him timidly, half daring, half apprehensive.

He was surprised at his own response; instead

of being delighted, he was embarrassed; he felt touched and troubled.

"What are you thanking me for?" he demanded, a little gruffly; "nothing. It is you who have done something, for a lonely man." He was going to say "a lonely old man," but changed his mind.

She put her hand on his, and he took it and thought how soft and warm it was, and at the same time he felt the strong clean bones, the nervous skeleton under the skin. A young woman's hand, firm and gentle: a promise . . .

"Max," she said hesitantly, "could I ask you something? You've been so good to me. . . ."

"What is it?" He smiled indulgently.

"I have only this one dress," she said.

"I see."

He felt disappointed and ashamed. So that was what she wanted of him—a dress; as though he were a wealthy patron, a butter-and-egg-man, a salesman from Chicago . . .

She searched his face with a troubled expression, and then shook her head. "No," she said; "that isn't what I meant. I only thought perhaps if I could have it cleaned. If you could afford it, I mean. These spots . . . I tried turpentine, but that only made them worse."

"Naturally," he exclaimed. "Turpentine? Good heavens!"

"It was all I could find," she said.

Well, he said to himself, to Max Loeb the painter. Why are you surprised? Couldn't you have noticed the spots? If you are going to take on something, do it at least like a man. This is not a Kiki from the Quarter, or a Solange who knows her way around. This is Miss Smith from Oregon City, who has only this one dress in which she has been sleeping on the beach and which is now even worse because of the turpentine.

"Of course," he said; "of course we can afford it. We will get the dress cleaned tomorrow."

CHAPTER 7

"I'll say this, that it's none of my business," Mrs. Bloemendal nevertheless declared, "but is it to be a permanent thing with the girl?"

All at once, to his surprise, Mr. Loeb found himself furiously angry. "Is there something permanent about borrowing a dress?" he asked. "She has only the one, and I am taking it out to be cleaned. If I had known there would be an investigation by the FBI—"

"And who's the FBI?" demanded Mrs. Bloemendal.

"She tried to clean it with turpentine," said Max stormily. "So now it is worse than ever, with rings."

"Well, now," said Hermione. "Doesn't she know any better?"

"She knows nothing," said Max. "She is practically an orphan."

Hermione sniffed a few times, gave a nervous cluck, and cleared her throat. "My clothes wouldn't fit her," she declared.

"Maybe not; but better to go out in than a towel."

"I'll see what I can do," said Hermoine. And as Max turned to leave, she added uncertainly: "Does she mean so much to you?"

"No," said Max. "And anyway, that has nothing to do with it."

As he walked back to the studio across the little patio, he thought: How do you like that? A man can't do a simple, manly thing without being asked what is behind it. As though something serious was involved . . . His steps slowed, and he stood still for a moment in the hot sun. Of course she means something to me, he said to himself; otherwise why would I? . . . But what did those words signify: 'so much'? An orphan, or almost, who drops in front of me like a sparrow with a broken wing; what is permanent about a sparrow? When the wing is healed, when she is ready, she will go.

But at the thought of her leaving he felt a sudden stab of anxiety. He saw himself alone again, and he experienced a sinking of the stomach. All right, he said to himself angrily, so I am not one hundred per cent unselfish. I am glad she is here, I have been happy since she came.

And when he entered the studio and saw her standing in the middle of the room, trying once more to iron out her dress, the sleeves of his old dressing gown rolled up on her thin, bare arms, he felt an emotion which surprised him by its strength and by its purity. It was not that of a father, or relative; it was the emotion of a stranger for an attractive young person of the opposite sex.

But it was also, at the same time, tender and innocent, and like the emotion with which Gounod's Faust first regarded Marguerite; *"Oh, merveille!"* he exclaimed, not realizing what was being offered. Or what there was to pay. How could he? —this same Faust—even if he had been able to remember from so long ago what it was like to be young? The raptures, the ardors, made gentle now, tempered by rheumatism and regret?

Max could remember, or thought he could; it seemed to him that in Halys—standing there with her young shoulders bent above the table in a small curve like a birch tree, over the creased and wrinkled dress and the hot iron—he saw all that was touching and vulnerable in youth, and at the same time something formidable, supple, pliant, and indomitable.

It is strange, he thought, how the mere sight of other people gives us courage. To be all alone in the world—that would be a terrifying experience;

even the lowest cell is aware of its companions, or at least it has the ability to divide itself in two and create a family. But imagine—if there were no one else, anywhere! no memory, even, of any human creature! Even the wild black hermit bee knows there are other bees somewhere, in the world, or in the next meadow. . . .

"Mrs. Bloemendal is going to lend you a dress," he said.

Halys straightened up slowly, and turned to him with a puzzled look. "Why?" she asked suspiciously; "when she doesn't like me?"

"She has nothing against you personally," said Max. "It is the situation which upsets her. She wanted to know if this was to be a—" He stopped suddenly.

"A what?" asked Halys.

"Well, nothing really," he said lamely. "She just wanted to know, that was all."

"I see," said Halys. "That's why I want to look for a job."

"It really isn't necessary," said Max unhappily. "She didn't mean . . ."

She wet her finger in her mouth and tested the iron. "I don't need her dress," she said. "I can iron this out so the worst part won't show."

"I was going to have it cleaned," said Max unhappily.

"After I get a job," she said, "I'll buy a brand-new dress."

"It is you who dislike her, I think," said Max slowly, "rather than the other way 'round. But why? And do you dislike me, too?"

"No," she said. She put the iron down, and turned to him and shook him in exasperation. "You mustn't say such things," she exclaimed. "You mustn't believe that, ever!"

A moment later, with a cry of anguish, she turned back to the table on which the hot iron, set down so hastily on the cloth, was filling the room with a smell of scorching.

"Now look what you've made me do!" she cried,

holding up the dress to the light, studying it with pursed lips, turning it anxiously this way and that. But actually very little harm had been done. "It looks a little toasted," she announced at last, "but I guess it won't show too much. Anyway, it will have to do."

But later, when Hermione came across the patio with one of her own dresses for her, she was as meek as a schoolgirl, and received it with a polite smile, and appeared to be actually grateful. It was quite a good dress, and she looked very well in it. "It's nice, really," she said, turning and revolving in front of the large and not very clean mirror which Max used from time to time to get a reverse view of his canvases. "Even if I don't fit into it very well."

She wasn't used to people being nice to her, and Hermione's kindness abashed her. On the other hand, if she was surprised, so was Hermione. Mrs. Bloemendal had no reason to like Miss Smith of Oregon City—though for that matter she had no reason to dislike her, either, without admitting something she didn't want to admit. But she felt sorry, despite herself, either for Halys or for Max, she wasn't sure which, or possibly both. The girl had been, after all, a member of the profession, or almost; anyway, Hermione knew what it was like to have nothing to wear, to have to look for a job in an old raincoat to cover the holes.

Or perhaps there was something else in it. . . . The girl was nubile, and marriageable; the sooner she found something to do, the sooner she'd be away from there. Unless, of course, it was to be something permanent after all; but in that case the battle was already lost. What battle she meant, she didn't know, and couldn't have explained; as far as she knew—or would admit to knowing—she had no desire to marry Max herself. But it was a comfort to have him there, behind the house.

And besides, there was something unseemly about a man his age and a young girl living together under one roof, no matter what they were —or weren't—up to. Perhaps "seemly" wasn't just what she meant, as a Catholic: the right way to say it was to say that they weren't adding to the treasury of merit, and weren't in a state of grace.

All of which could be rectified, in time, perhaps.

Max looked at Mrs. Bloemendal, and at Halys pirouetting before the glass, with approval. Always in the end there was something about people which warmed his heart no matter how doubtful he might be of humanity on the whole; something that demanded a certain amount of admiration, and even a kind of reverence. When he saw men and women being happy and being good to one another, he felt a rush almost of delight: that was how it ought to be, that was as natural as . . . as what? All other creatures stung, pecked, tore, slashed, chewed, or swallowed one another, which seemed much more like an accident than kindness or the position of the galaxies. People, being kind, being gentle . . . Maybe God wasn't in them, but there was certainly something more than earth!

"I thought perhaps," said Hermione suddenly, "that you'd have dinner with me tonight. It's Friday, so it's fish. . . ."

And as she waited for their answer, wondering meanwhile what had got into her, she revised her menu in her mind: the one small Rex sole wouldn't do, she would have to go back to the market and change it for a red snapper, and stuff and bake it.

"Why," said Max slowly, "we'd like to very much. At what time?"

"At six, I think," said Hermione vaguely from the doorway, "or seven." There were too many imponderables for her to be sure which. Let me see, she thought as she hurried down the street, how long does it take to bake a snapper? An hour? Forty-five minutes?

For dinner that night Halys wore the new dress. She had brushed out her hair, and she had found a piece of ribbon to tie in it; but Max wore his usual working trousers and corduroy jacket. He didn't say so, but he had a feeling that he shouldn't make too much of it, that he ought to appear, at least, to take the evening in stride. It wasn't the first time he had dined with Mrs. Bloemendal, but it was the first time he had ever brought anyone else to dinner with him. He didn't want her to think that—to him, at least—it was an occasion.

But the truth was, it was an occasion, because for the first time in a long while he was going somewhere with someone, and not alone.

It wasn't entirely easy for Hermione, but she did her best, first with the fish, and then with the situation. To Halys, anyway, the fish was delicious. "That's the thing," she said, "about a real stove, you can cook on it. That is, of course," she added a little confusedly, "I can't; but if you can, I mean."

"Anyone can cook," Max declared, "though"—with a courtly bow to his hostess—"I must admit this snapper is very delicate. On a gas ring, however, one is handicapped. With a real stove I could make you a bouillabaisse . . . that is, if I had the necessary ingredients. One needs merlan, and octopus. The best bouillabaisse is to be found at Scandia, a restaurant to which my friend Herzig once took me. You see, I have known rich people in my life. A charmer, this Herzig; a Viennese, like myself, at least by inclination, but more American, being born here and working at Warner Brothers. I remember that the restaurant was very crowded, with people waiting for tables; but Herzig had no trouble, they knew him at Scandia. That was the only time I ate there; it was delicious, but in general beyond me.

"Do you know the place I like to eat best? It is beside a little round ring of concrete on the sands at Playa del Rey. Next week we will all go there for supper, and the hamburgers will be on me. Made with mustard, with sauces, with chopped onion; very spectacular."

Hermione gave a slight, inaudible sigh. She was doing all she could; the trouble seemed to lie in the fact that she wasn't sure of what it really was that she was trying to do. So far, apparently, she hadn't convinced Mr. Loeb of anything; all she'd done was to get herself invited to a beach picnic.

And Mr. Loeb was still bent, as far as she could see, on looking after the girl from Oregon, or from nowhere. Nobody had looked after Hermione since Mr. Bloemendal died. Was that what she wanted?

to be taken care of? It sounded ridiculous, but it felt a little bit like it.

"Drink your coffee," she said to Max, "before it gets cold."

CHAPTER 8

MAN has but little wisdom—only enough to advise his neighbors, never enough for himself. For one thing, nothing ever comes at him head-on, in full view; it is always from the side where everyone can get a good look at it except the victim. Anyone else, then, can tell him what is coming, and what to do about it, but the poor fellow himself has no idea of what he's up against, and goes about making excuses and inventing fairytales until it is too late for anything but history.

So with Max in the days which followed. For an old painter in his sixties to fall in love with a waif like Halys was not to be thought of; it was purely nonsensical, in the sense of being the opposite of sensible. So, Max told himself that what he felt for Halys was something altogether different, and not love at all. In a way he was right: in love everything is always different.

Because love is, after all, only a word. It is an idea: one thing and many things, and not a thing at all, only a name for something. It comes and it goes, almost at will; it changes light and color, it is chameleon; it develops, deteriorates, is remembered, forgotten; it lasts forever or for a day, and it goes equally and always by the one name: love. It is a hunger, and, like any hunger, those who experience it believe that it can never end. Yet, like other hungers, it has been known to.

Max remembered how it used to be: how a

woman's scent, the curve of her waist, the warmth of her mouth raised the man in him. And how the great lovers of history had once seemed like heroes and heroines. When I was young, he thought, they filled my heart with wonder and pity. It has been a long time, a long time! He no longer dreamed of Isolde or Juliet; and scarcely remembered the dark-haired Suzanne in the little shop in the rue du Bac. She had seemed to him for a whole year like the Lady of the Camellias.

When I was young, he mused, the beauty of women wounded me. I looked at them, and I wounded them with my eyes. A force came out of me, it held the air between us like a magnet. There was something between us like anguish. But when I look at Halys, it is without force, without any wounds; the air between us sparkles with sunlight.

It was not the same thing as anguish at all; he didn't even know if he should call it love. But when he thought of going without her, he suddenly felt lost and woeful.

Suzanne would be an old woman by now, if she wasn't already dead. And what was Juliet but a rebellious teenager? A fifteen-year-old, or thirteen if one was to believe the chronicles—and in love with a schoolboy, besides! Not that a seventeen-year-old Montague was ever likely to be at school, except in some lady's bedchamber.

The old stories, the love stories, were always about the young. It was only lately that older men were considered proper objects of romance—or even, sometimes, marriage.

Occasionally his thoughts grew daring; he thought of Halys in bed with him, warm instead of cold, gentle and willing. . . . When she was fifty, he would be ninety-something. Still, people lived longer nowadays, with orange juice and anti-biotics—longer still if they had someone to look after them. Or, perhaps (it had a nicer sound), if they had someone to look after; someone who turned to them for protection, from the world, from loneliness and want. To have someone to look after—that was it; it gave a man a sense of manhood, it gave a man a glow.

He thought of Rembrandt and Saskia, of Modigliani and his Jeanne, of Renoir and Alice Charigat. To have a wife was not altogether a bad thing for a painter. He and Halys could rent a stove; and he did not doubt that he could teach her to cook.

But then he would have a moment of panic, and think. Have I lost my mind? In the first place, she would never have me; and in the second, what am I thinking of? A young creature like that! Am I so attractive?

Actually, Halys didn't think of him as unattractive, or as attractive, either; he was, simply, someone who had been good to her, a man—not a young man, but what young man had ever been kind? Not Jon, certainly, and no one else she could think of.

And as she went about the city in the next few days, following the *Help Wanted* ads in the paper, she thought about Max a good deal. He was no ordinary person, such as she had met on her travels: he was gentle and kind, he was a painter, an artist, a man of the world who knew how to cook an octopus. And he had been born and had lived abroad, seven thousand miles from Oregon City. It all added up in her mind, if not to glory, at least to refinement and the advantages.

And she was grateful. A shy, warm feeling of gratitude suffused her like a blush. To be cared for by such a man! That didn't happen all the time to everybody. What a compliment!

It was in this state of mind, and in Mrs. Bloemendal's dress, that Halys stopped in at the market to buy, with the money given her that morning by Mr. Loeb, a box of Fig Newtons and a small carton of milk for her lunch. She knew she had no business trying to eat it there, behind a row of canned soups and vegetables, but she didn't think it would be Jon who caught her at it and told her so. "Go away," she hissed at him. "You haven't seen me."

"Well," he said uncomfortably, "I have; and you'd better take it out of here, and pay for it."

"I'll pay for it when I'm through," said Halys with as much dignity as she could muster with her mouth full of Fig Newtons. "I didn't think you'd be so disloyal!"

Jon stared at her in amazement. "Disloyal!" he croaked. "To who?"

"To Max," she said accusingly. "After the way he's helped you, and everything."

"I don't see what Max has to do with it," said Jon. "You come in here and eat and drink like it was a restaurant or something. . . ." His eyes widened, and he looked at her sharply. "You've got a new dress," he said. "Who gave it to you?"

"Do you like it?" she asked anxiously, spilling a little milk as she twirled around on her toes to show it off. "Mrs. Bloemendal loaned it to me."

"It doesn't fit," said Jon judiciously. "It's too big for you."

Halys gave him a stony glance. "At least," she said, "she tries to help."

"Well, heck," said Jon; "what are you so sorry for yourself all the time for?"

"I'm not sorry for myself," said Halys. "I simply said—"

"You'd think nobody ever did anything for you in your life," said Jon.

"Nobody ever did," said Halys simply. "Except Max."

So now it's first names, he thought: Max. "And me," he said stubbornly. "Max and me. The two of us."

"You?" she cried scornfully. "What did you do?"

"Well—I was there, wasn't I?"

"Sure; you were there. So were a lot of other people. They didn't talk to me, though. Do you know what you said?"

Jon looked down at his feet. "Well, no," he said uncomfortably. "I guess I don't, exactly."

"You said: 'It can't be that bad,'" said Halys. "You said: 'Excuse me, I have to go to the gent's.'" He tried to look at her, but she stared him down. "So now I can't eat my lunch here," she said.

"Well, you can't!" he complained. "It'd be worth my job if they caught you."

"I don't know why I came in here at all," said Halys. "I could have gone to lots of other places."

"I wish you had," said Jon earnestly. "I do sincerely."

"I don't think I want any of this," said Halys; and, thrusting the Fig Newtons and the milk into Jon's arms, she turned and hurried down the aisle and out through the turnstile to the street. "I didn't buy anything," she said to the checker at the gate, holding up her empty hands. There was a drop of milk on her chin, but nobody noticed it.

Jon looked gloomily down at the box of Fig Newtons. He guessed they'd have to be his lunch. He hated Fig Newtons.

All Halys wanted to do was go home to Max. The thought of trudging up and down bright, dusty streets all afternoon, up and down cold, musty, plaster-smelling stairs, hoping for that one miraculous job, that possible living, seemed at the moment almost more than she could bear. And why, after all, did she have to? Max wanted her to stay, he had said so. And what was wrong with that arrangement? He couldn't pay her for posing for him, but she didn't have any expenses; she got a home and her meals and the loan of a dress from Mrs. Bloemendal, and lunch money, like today.

How good it was and what a comfort to know that the studio was there—if not cool, at least shady in the hot summer weather, and the mock-orange smelling in the sun, and the jasmine at night. A place to rest, and hide—from unfriendly people, from an unloving world.

Who cared if she got a job or not? The mayor of Los Angeles? Why did she care so much herself, when no one else did? Not her mother, far away in the north with a bottle in her hand. Not Jon, certainly . . .

What had she ever done to make him dislike her so much? Sometimes he almost seemed to hate her. Well, if that was the case, two could play . . . Oh, what difference did it make? Jon was nothing to her: a boy, a sulky boy.

Max was sitting before his easel when she got

back, his shoulders hunched up around his ears, and all the rest of him drooping, staring at the empty canvas in front of him with a curious, lost expression on his face. "I didn't find anything," she said. "I got tired of looking."

He seemed to draw in a long breath like a sigh, and turned and rummaged in the box where he kept his pieces of charcoal. "I am glad," he said. "Now we can get to work."

She felt a sharp drop of spirits. Was that all he had to say: now we can get to work? All of a sudden she was tired; she felt that she looked a sight, her borrowed dress didn't fit, she was hot, her hair was untidy . . . She was too young to end her days like that, before her life was even begun! He didn't really care for her, he only wanted her to pose for him, he didn't love her. It was a business arrangement. Very well, she would make it so.

"I shall have to be paid," she said.

Max looked her over slowly; his face was without expression. "Yes," he said at last; "of course. How much will you charge?"

How much? All at once she felt her throat tighten up; she wanted to cry. She shook her head mutely. Nothing, she was saying soundlessly inside; nothing. I love you. That's why I'm staying.

Instead, all she could do was hold out to him the coins in her purse, the ones left over from the market. "Never mind," said Max gently; "we will talk about it later. Meanwhile, there is an avocado in the icebox, with oil and vinegar; because it looks as if you hadn't had your lunch."

CHAPTER 9

ALWAYS in August the earth, circling in space on its Grand Tour of the heavens, encounters the Perseids, and for a few nights stars streak across the sky, and lovers, lying on their backs among the sandy dunes of Cape Cod and in the dew-drenched fields of Indiana, watch the silver rain, and make their wishes.

Max, Halys, Jon, and Mrs. Bloemendal sat beside their fire at Playa del Rey. It was the hour after sunset, and not yet night; the pale moon was straight up overhead, three-quarters full, there was still some milky blue in the sky, and only the evening star hung in the west, yellow as candlelight.

Max was thinking about his picture; already he had it in his mind, he knew what he wanted to do. And on a block of drawing paper, with a soft pencil, he was making a sketch of Halys as she sat in front of the fire, her arms over her knees, staring dreamily into the flames. He had studied her in this same pose before, it presented no new problems: what he wanted to get was the light, and for this he made notes in a kind of shorthand of his own, and notes also for the background. It was all in his head, but he wanted it written down, in case he should ever forget. For instance: the firelight threw a green shadow onto Halys's face; that was an interesting thing to analyze.

They were talking about certain books Mrs.

Bloemendal had taken home to read from the Santa Monica library, to which she had a card. "I don't know," she said in a puzzled voice: "they tell me it's realism. We had another name for it when I was on the stage." She smiled timidly, and sighed, and looked into the fire. "The funny thing is," she said, "that nobody talks nicely to anybody any more. In books, I mean. They just . . . well . . . do it."

She blushed a little, and looked around defiantly. "With Mr. Bloemendal," she said, "we used to discuss the building business afterwards. Or people we knew; things like that. Family things: you know, like friends."

She took a quick breath, and suddenly grew embarrassed. "I hope I'm not shocking anybody," she said.

"Oh, no," said Halys. "Not at all."

Just speak for yourself, thought Jon; speak for yourself.

"Realism," grumbled Max, sketching away. "You call it realism what we get? Is a bone with gristle on it realism? Maybe—for a cemetery. Do you know what true realism is? It is the bone inside the flesh, under the living tissue: paint that, or write about it! Even in the newspapers you can find out what is going on with our artists, or sometimes in a magazine at the barber shop. Do you know what I think about these books you read? They are not like life, because in life everybody is not such a good-for-nothing."

"I know a few," said Jon.

"Maybe what I mean," said Max, "is not so much a no-good, but a bum. Excuse the expression," he said to Hermione.

"Not at all," said Mrs. Bloemendal elegantly. "Get on with it."

"When I was young," said Max, "if you were sick they took you to a doctor, they didn't put you on the stage. Even in Vienna; even in Austria."

Mrs. Bloemendal nodded enthusiastically. "I know what you mean," she said. "Yes, indeed."

"And if all you thought about was drink," continued Max, "or what was under women's skirts, that did not by itself make a hero of you in a book."

Jon looked secretly over at Halys. The girl still sat in the position in which Max had been sketching her. He couldn't tell whether she heard what they were saying or not; she seemed to be dreaming, the clean, taut line of her back bent in a gentle curve, her arms over her knees. There was no telling what she was thinking. I never heard the old man like this, Jon thought; and that landlady of his! What's got into them?

"Well," said Hermione defiantly, "it does now. I was reading this book where a young man wants to be a writer. What I mean is, he wants to write books. Only—all he is, is what you called him; a drunken bum. Just the same, he's the hero in the book, except for a friend of his, and this one another like himself. And I couldn't find so much as a page where anybody said a nice word to anybody else."

"As I say," rumbled Max, "I don't read very much, only the newspapers. In the newspapers, nobody's a hero."

"You can be a hero," said Halys suddenly, "by rescuing somebody from the sea."

"Sure," said Jon; "like this girl I read about and the shark. Or from a fire; you go in there and pull them out."

"Have you ever tried it?" asked Max gently. "I believe that when you see a wall of flame, or fifty yards of icy water, with a shark at the other end—"

"Drowning people grab at you," said Halys. "They try to choke you."

"That's right," said Jon flatly. "They grab at you."

He threw a quick, meaningful glance at her from hooded eyes, but she didn't appear to notice. She spoke in a low voice, as though out of a dream. "It's black and cold out there," she said, "and all alone, and you get frightened. If you haven't ever been frightened, you don't know . . . You grab at whatever there is."

"That's what I mean," said Jon.

Max looked up from his sketching, a puzzled frown on his usually mild face. Was there something underneath this talk that he didn't understand, something he'd missed? Something between these two? Jon in particular . . . he'd never heard him so sharp. Or was it bitter? And Halys; had he imagined it? or had she sounded bitter, too? And somehow defensive?

And, looking at them both, he saw for the first time that their faces were closed—not only against him, but against each other. Here, he thought; here; what is going on?

He put down his sketch pad in a hurry. "Come," he said as heartily as he could; "let us put on the hamburgers."

For a while the three of them, Max, Jon, and Hermione, were busy with the wire grill and the round red patties of meat. Hermione had brought some corn, which was dropped in among the embers, each ear still wrapped in its own green, drying sheath. Only Halys sat watching, not moving, a faraway look on her face. It was neither friendly nor unfriendly; it was lonely, and indifferent.

The falling grease brought little spurts of yellow flame from the fire. "Not too much," said Max anxiously; "once meat is cooked too long, nothing can uncook it. Who likes it rare?"

"Just so long as I don't see the blood," said Hermione.

"And yet," said Max with mock severity, "you belong to the blood-thirstiest species on earth; the only difference between you and a tiger is that someone else slices the meat for you and carves the flesh from the bones. After the roast is prepared, you will eat it with a sense of innocence, like broccoli.

"Don't feel too badly about it," he added, as Hermione tossed her head indignantly: "every creature on earth is the victim of something; even man. One never knows what is coming. Only a few weeks ago a bird, a young bluejay—a female, I think—pursued by heaven knows what terror, or out of pure stupidity, or perhaps exhilaration, flew head-on against the glass window of my studio, and fell unconscious to the ground. Nearby, in one of your own bushes, her mate—or possibly an aunt or an uncle—gave anxious chirks and fluttered his wings without being the slightest use to her. Birds cannot help one another, they can only worry and sympathize. Without a thumb and the knowledge of how to use it, one is very vulnerable on this earth. Only man can help his brother man."

"For a price," said Jon.

Max looked at him keenly from under lowered brows. "Yes," he said slowly; "perhaps. For a price. We all want something."

But he was waiting to hear what Jon would say. "I have nothing," said Jon, "and I don't want anything. I have what I paint; what I paint belongs to me, I made it, and it's mine." He looked around defiantly. "That's why I don't paint faces," he declared. "I don't want a face to belong to me."

"You would find it a great comfort sometimes," said Max, looking at Halys. He continued: "There are some consolations, after all, in the world." But Halys didn't look up, and after a moment he went on. "The fact is, the world is not a gentle place, Hermione."

"Don't I know it," said Mrs. Bloemendal.

"And man," Max continued, "is not gentle, either. It is not necessary to go into the many cruel things he does, not only to the other animals, but to his fellow men. Even his young commit murder, in a fit of petulance, or because they think they are being held back from the enjoyments of being grown-up. And yet—of all living creatures man is the only one capable of love, the only one able to feel pity. Isn't that strange, Hermione? What's more, in spite of his nature, he often wishes that he was pure and good. What can you make of such a contradiction? For whatever there is in it, it's as near as I can get to man's soul."

"The Church would put you closer to it, then," said Hermione, picking up her hamburger. "The way you talk, it's like you thought the world was mad."

"I'm not sure it isn't mad," said Max somberly: "the human part of it, anyway. Certainly the insects appear to carry on as usual, with their customary imperturbability. But men? When I see sculptures made out of nuts and bolts, out of old tin cans or slabs of concrete, paintings made up of a few straight lines and some blobs of colors, operas and symphonies composed of harsh cries and screams, then I don't know; I am inclined to expect the worst. What future is there for man in the world unless God is looking out for him?"

"But God is," said Hermione, smearing butter on her corn.

"Yet we must face the fact," mused Max, "that no one could possibly be satisfied to have created such a world."

"Who said He was satisfied?" demanded Hermione.

Max smiled a little. "You are right," he said. "Only lovers can imagine that He is satisfied. Still," he added, "the truly God-fearing Christian must believe that God is not a helpless noodle, and that everything transpires according to His will.

"And that," he concluded soberly, "is just the trouble. Because we know that everything is moving around us at enormous speeds, flying away from us, or rushing at us from every direction; and only we, in our separate, lonely, singular lives, do not seem to be going anywhere."

"There is nowhere to go," said Halys simply.

"There must be," said Max; "if only because, where everything moves, to stand still is impractical, and not very gay. And on the other hand, to move toward madness . . ."

It was Halys who echoed the age-old cry. "Maybe God is mad," she said. "Did anyone ever think of that?"

Mrs. Bloemendal gazed at her in consternation. The poor soul, she needs the comforts of the Church, she thought; but there was no way to tell her so, and no need, really, what with all the saints and angels standing by, and they wiser than she.

Always in August the earth, circling in space, encounters the Perseids; the stars, streaking through
the sky, reflect an ordered universe in which no
sparrow falls unremarked.

CHAPTER 10

AFTER supper, Max and Hermione stretched out on a blanket beside the dying fire, and Jon and Halys, without saying anything to each other, got up and started up the beach more or less together, Halys striding along in the way she had, erect, and toes first, like a cat, and Jon kicking his feet in the sand,

and coming down on his heels. The yellow fire-light dwindled away behind them, leaving small circles of gold in the sand no brighter than the windows of the houses above them on the hill. A star blazed for a moment across the sky, falling in a long arc, and Halys said: "Make a wish."

She turned and put her hand out, and he caught up with her and took hold of it for a moment and then let it go again. They went on side by side, their feet half in the water as it ran up the beach and half in the wet sand. The water was cold; it looked black and deep out there where the waves rose almost unseen and rolled in and broke in a long crash of night-gray foam, and ran up over their feet.

"All that about spiders and wasps a while back," said Jon; "it's on his mind. It's funny, too, because the way he paints it isn't like that at all; you'd think he saw everything through rosy glasses." He kicked at a gobbet of foam and lifted it into the air.

"He does," she said. "That's how he sees it."

She seemed to have nothing more to say at the moment, and they walked along in silence for a while. Jon glanced at her from time to time; in the night-darkness and the star-shine he couldn't make out her expression very well, only the slender, erect, pliant, arrogant figure and the tilt of her head. He thought that her profile looked stern, even angry, and this puzzled him. What has she got to be angry about? he thought.

Where the beach curved in a little, she turned away from the water and walked by herself up the sloping sand into the darkness, and began to slip out of her dress. "I'm going in," she called back to him. He could see the white glimmer of her body as she let her slip fall, but it was all shadowy and indistinct. He felt his heart beat, and he swallowed air.

"Well, wait a minute," he said. And he added uncertainly: "Do you know how to swim?"

Her reply was scornful. "Of course," she said, poised for a moment on tiptoe in the night-misty air. "Did you think I was going to drown myself?"

A moment later she was running down the sand, as light as a sandpiper, and had flung herself under a wave.

Jon undressed slowly; he felt lonely and naked and afraid. He went hesitatingly down to the sea, which stretched out before him dim and secret and covered with silver sequins of moonlight. The air was cold on his skin, he thought of all the dangerous unknown creatures in those black waters; as Max said, it was different when you were face to face with it. He went in slowly and gingerly, the water curling and surging against his naked thighs and up over his belly, hissing at him like a snake; it was strong, it pulled and tugged at him, a tumble of foam came rolling and crashing at him, he bent and went under it, and then he was floating, rising and falling, out beyond the surf, free of the fall and foam and follow of the waves, and feeling clean and easy.

Halys was there, somewhere in the darkness among those lifting swells; and suddenly, with a sense of being lost, and in a kind of panic, more

than anything in the world he wanted to find her
—had to find her, another creature like himself,
another human in that lonely element with its
surges, its eddies and currents, moving in cataracts,
in great streaming tides far out across the world.
"Halys," he called; "Halys!"

She answered him at once from nearby, coming
over a rising comber, her hair floating out behind
her. He couldn't see her very well, only her small,
pale face above the black water, and the white
shimmer of her bare shoulders. Her eyes, he
thought, were as dark as the sea. "I thought maybe
you'd got lost or something," he said lamely.

"Did you?" She looked at him coolly, paddling
on her stomach like a seal. "Well, I didn't," she
said. "Not this time."

What did she mean, not this time? He didn't
know what she meant. "It's cold," he said. "Maybe
we better go back in."

She didn't answer; she turned and swam away.
She didn't swim particularly well, she swam the
way a child would swim who had learned in a

public pool. But Jon didn't swim any better; he was a creek-and-river thrasher.

He turned back to the beach, watching fearfully over his shoulder for a breaking wave, and made his way up the sloping sand to his clothes. There was no way to dry himself, and he stood there shivering, holding his shirt and trousers in his hand and peering around him anxiously at the shadows. He didn't want anybody to see him like that. He had a moment of grim humor, utterly unlike him. It's not a thumb at all, he thought, makes a man feel safe: it's a pair of pants.

And then, without his seeing her come, Halys was beside him. "Here," she said, tossing him her slip; "dry yourself off." She had her dress on again, it clung to her wet body like a flowing of wind. "Thanks," he said, and took it, and turned away to dry himself, not knowing what it was.

She didn't stay to watch him; he could have spared himself his modesty. He found her sitting back from the beach in the shadow of a small ledge or overhang which seemed to make a kind of cave in the cliff behind her. Overhead the traffic flowed along the Vista del Mar in an endless whisper, lights blazed, and horns hooted, but where they were there was only the dark, the dim ocean and the night sky, the nibbled moon and the stars. He gave her back her slip, and she thanked him almost absently and let it fall in the sand. "You know," he said, "I don't get you at all. I don't know do you hate me, or what?"

"Why should I hate you?" she asked. "I thought it was the other way 'round."

"You mean me?" he said, and lied a little. "Why, no. I wouldn't have any reason to."

"No," she agreed; "why would you?"

She pointed almost indifferently to the darker shadow of the overhang behind her. "That's where I slept," she said. "Right there." Her voice registered nothing.

"You know," he said, using his fingers like a rake in the sand, sifting the cold sand through his fingers, "I tried to get you a job at the market. But there wasn't anything."

She glanced at him in surprise. "I didn't know that," she said. She was silent a moment, looking out to sea with a puzzled expression. "Thanks, anyway," she said at last.

"For what?" he asked. "I didn't do anything."

They were both silent, listening to the hushed roar of the surf, and to the whisper of the cars overhead. "Look," he said after a while; "you got any plans?"

"No," she said, half drowsily; "have you?"

"Well, no," he said uncertainly. "I didn't mean anything like that. What I was wondering was if you and the old man—"

She sat up sharply, outraged, and coiled to strike. "Me and *who?*" she asked.

"Max," said Jon hastily. "I meant Max. If you and he . . . well . . . were . . ."

"Were what?"

"Are you going to marry him?" he asked in a rush, and looked away, down the beach.

She stared at him wide-eyed, in stony silence. What right had he to ask such a question? Something that hadn't even entered her head until that moment. "Maybe," she said coolly, with a taste of bitterness in her mouth. "If he asks me to."

"I see," he said dully. "Well . . ."

He had no idea what she was feeling. She looked so gentle sitting there, with such small sweet wrists, and her young body soft and tender, and her sea-wet hair down over her shoulders, all fragrant . . . "If that's what you want," he said, "I guess that's what you want."

"Yes," she said. "I guess it is."

"I hope you'll be happy," he said. "I wish you every happiness."

"Thank you," she said coldly. "In case he asks me."

"In case he asks you," he echoed. "Yes—well, in case he doesn't . . ."

She watched him—wary, alert, waiting for what he was going to say—sensing his hesitation, seeing suddenly for the first time his aloneness. She hadn't thought of him being like herself. He seemed to her, for the moment, as defenseless in the world as a caterpillar; one step, and that was the end of him. And she felt sorry for him, in a way she hadn't expected: it was a warm feeling, almost amused, and full of pity. "Yes?" she said, "in case he doesn't?" At the same time her heart beat a little faster.

He shook his head dispiritedly. "Nothing," he said.

"It's only . . ."

His eyes seemed enormous in the darkness, and full of some kind of grief. "Look," he said: "sometimes you don't see things till it's too late. You don't see them right. . . . Like I'd try to paint the moon on that water, and think it was silver instead of blue. At least . . . it's . . . a kind of blue, I guess. It's something about what's down there, underneath; I don't know how to say it. I mean sort of at the bottom of things, in your heart."

He paused, embarrassed at what he had already said, and at a loss to know how to go on. Once again she thought how the wrong word, the wrong step, would crush him. "I think I know what you mean," she said gently; "and thank you." But she didn't know; she had no idea of what he was trying to say.

Neither did he. But he leaned forward all at once and kissed her clumsily on the cheek, and she, startled, shrank back, and then jumped to her feet. "It's time we got out of here," she said. "I'm freezing."

They walked back in silence, the same way they had come, with Jon lagging behind. And each, as they drew nearer their own fire, felt more and more indignant, without knowning exactly why—Halys blaming Jon for kissing her the way he did, so suddenly, by surprise, and for being unkind, for being young . . . more than anything else for being young, and why did he have to be so unkind?—and Jon at Halys for taking it the way she did, and making him feel guilty. At least, that is what they told themselves. But underneath, Jon was angry at himself for his bumbling confusion, and Halys at her own dark, troubling thoughts and troubled feelings.

For that very reason she was sweet to Max as she dried herself off by the fire; and for his own reasons Jon was silent and unresponsive. Mrs. Bloemendal looked at them and sighed; when they'd gone off together she had thought it so right, and obviously it hadn't been, even though they had been swimming apparently with nothing on.

Unfortunately, there was nothing particularly familiar, or even friendly, in swimming at night in the nude; she had often done it herself when she was young, first with other people, and later with Mr. Bloemendal. In the dark all cats were gray; and cold sea water had a very sobering effect. The girl, she noticed, was carrying her slip, but perhaps she had used it as a towel.

All this Max saw also, with a certain heaviness of heart. He sensed that there had been a quarrel; what troubled him was the thought that people who are indifferent to each other usually don't quarrel, there is nothing to quarrel about.

He was an old hand at things like that: things

of the heart, sudden storms, silences, the speaking look. And that, of course, was the rub—that one word: old. There was no way for age to compete with youth. Forty years ago—or even twenty—it would have been different; no girl would have slept alone on a sofa in his room. Not for ten days, not for a week, not for any reason. If he had had no success with her, he would have asked her to move out. But now what he wanted was something else, something gentler and kinder, both from him and from her. And that was where he was handicapped. A man who wanted kindness was at a disadvantage, he could only give what he hoped to receive, there was no way for him to use force, or to force his way. At his age he couldn't creep—however timidly—into a girl's bed without having to apologize . . . without leaving himself open to ridicule, or to the possibility of disgusting her and losing her altogether. Unless she loved him, of course; but that was quite a different story.

It didn't seem likely. Still, stranger things had happened.

CHAPTER 11

AFTER that evening on the beach, Jon stayed away
from the studio, and Max was obliged to admit—
to himself, at least—that he was relieved. He felt
that in Jon's eyes he had lost his standing in the
world: he was no longer a teacher, someone to
look up to; he was a competitor.

It was an uncomfortable position; he imagined

that to anyone on the outside he must appear more than a little ridiculous. But when he thought about it, he found some consolation in the fact that he was an artist; he was Max Loeb, whose pictures had been exhibited in Paris and in New York, and about whom the art critic of *The New York Times* had said: "The painting *Solange at the Window* by Max Loeb has a certain quality of emotion." Under it Max had scrawled a single French word. But his canvases hung in the living rooms of half a dozen houses, and also in a museum in Basel, and in Newark, New Jersey.

He set himself to work: he started his picture of the beach at night, painting from memory and from his notes and sketches, and for a while he felt young and vibrant, and full of the old wild hope and enthusiasm. Halys posed for him while he worked on the figure in the foreground, though he had studied and sketched her so many times that he could almost have painted her from memory.

It was a dangerous mood to be in; it wasn't hard to imagine himself back in the past and—as in the past—to find himself in love. And where this same euphoria turns some men rowdy and faunlike, in Max it had the effect of making him gay and merry. He charmed Halys, it was easy for her to find the studio more attractive than ever, and to think herself, also, in love.

Or perhaps they were. They were happy with each other and they took comfort in being together. Halys was relaxed, at moments almost indolent, the past forgotten; if there was a future, it was no concern of hers. She rested in the present, content to pose when Max asked her to, to housekeep in a vague way, to walk with him in the evening, to drowse and dream. Max imagined the future to be full of promise.

And so, for a while, it seemed to be. A small gallery in Santa Monica sold one of his canvases of the Malibu hills at sunset, looking inland from the sea, and there was an inquiry from a retired chiropractor who thought of having his portrait done. A group of ladies who called themselves the Julia A. Moore Club, in honor of the Sweet Singer of Michigan, wrote to ask him if he would address them; they were interested in hearing about the artist's life, in Paris and Greenwich Village. The fee they offered was small, but it could lead to other lectures, and included a collation.

As a result of all this, Max bought Halys a washable cotton dress at J. C. Penney's for $12.98, and purchased two tickets to the Hollywood Bowl.

They sat high up in the stands with the cool blue night over them. The ground ran up steeply behind them; on all sides the Hollywood hills rose about them, darker than the sky, folding away into the distance dimmer than the air. Below them the shining white shell of the stage opened like a lily in a pool; the great lighted cross of the Passion Play gleamed on a neighboring hill; a few stars shone in the hollow sky crisscrossed by the red beams of warning searchlights. The sound of traffic on Highland beyond the trees rose in a hum of tires, and mingled with the steady flow of voices and the shuffle of feet as the audience flooded upward from the parks and foyers.

Halys was enchanted by it all—by the people, the lights, the glowing shell below them, the night-blue sky above, a lonely plane buzzing between the red beams like a lost bee, and the great golden moon rising, finally, behind the trees—and the music . . . first the players tuning their instruments, making that careless, exciting, eager sound; then the solemn hush, and finally the music itself, rising through the empty air, sweeping through the lonely dark around her in which she sat among thousands without knowing they were there.

She had no idea of what the music was. She closed her eyes and let herself be swept off into a place all her own, a sea of dreaming; with streams of rapture running through it. When she opened her eyes, the hills, the sky, the glowing bowl beneath her were still in her dream.

During the intermission Max took her for a walk along the promenade and through the foyers, and pointed out the notables: Van Johnson, carroty, freckled, and kind—a much bigger man than she had expected; the tall, gray-haired composer

Richard Hageman, and his wife, the gentle, white-haired Castelnuovo-Tedesco behind his thick glasses, the tiny, dynamic Stravinsky. Halys gazed at them stupidly, aware mostly of the ebb and flow of bodies all around her, the lights, the cold night air, the odor of pop corn and hot dogs, the nicker of voices and the rustle of feet. Back in her seat again, she forgot about them, and gave herself to the dream.

And she was still in it when the concert was over and they were hurrying down the ramps with the descending stream of people. And in the deeper dark of the parking lot where Max had left his battered car, finding herself close beside him, still in the lovely, lonely place, still in the spell, she pulled his face down to hers and in the most natural way kissed him on the mouth.

He was considerably shaken. So much so, that he made no effort to clasp her, but climbed speechlessly into the car and started the motor. She seemed almost unaware of him, or of what she had done. There were no sideways looks, no whispered

confidences; she sat in her corner of the seat, relaxed and silent, staring vaguely before her, and
with a faint smile around her lips.

They were a long time getting out of the park;
at one point, stopped for a while in traffic, he laid
his hand on hers; she returned its pressure so
gently that he felt she scarcely knew it was there.

He drove slowly and badly. At Franklin he
turned right, and wished he had gone straight
on to Fountain. He forgot to take Santa Monica
or Olympic, but went all the way west on Wilshire,
and then south on Lincoln, the long way home.
And all the while his thoughts either raced dizzily,
or else stood stock still—only to be off again, and
then go blank. Part of the time he smiled a little,
in a vacant way; once or twice he found himself
clenching his jaws as though to stop a shivering.
He was cold, exultant, and afraid; frightened, ex-
cited, hot, incredulous, and deeply moved.

And Halys? She was innocent and free and
happy. She had been bathed in music and in the
night; she had taken part in a ritual of beauty, and

she loved . . . someone. At that moment she felt that she loved Max with all her heart; he too, in her dream, was free, not made of flesh, and innocent. She could have given herself to him in a kiss, tender and delicate; she could have died for him, or she could have baked him a cherry pie if she had known how. The only thing she couldn't do was tell him why, when at home he turned to take her in his arms, she took sudden fright and stiffened and backed away; or why, later, alone in her bed in the dark, she wept and thought of small defenseless things such as caterpillars.

Moonlight filled the room, and from his bed Max stared upward at the ceiling, and tried to fight down the heavy feeling in his heart, the sense of grief and doubt. He brought all his knowledge to bear on his situation; he ranged back through his past, to try to find a parallel. There was none. One moment hot, he thought, and the next cold; I have been there before, but with a difference, another type altogether, full-bosomed and tempestuous. On that occasion, after the cold came the hot again, and this time scalding!

But this was something else. It is not a question of conquest, he thought, because she does not wish to be conquered. And yet, she loves me, I am sure of it. In her own way, perhaps—but the kiss she gave me was not that of a niece. It was warm, there was love in it . . . or did she seem to hold back a little? Well, perhaps that was natural.

He remembered his friend, the sculptor Borosov, who had married a schoolgirl in his fiftieth year, and had gone on to win the Prix Dreyfus and to place a bronze in the Luxembourg. He tried to remember what had become of Helene Borosov after her husband's death; he thought she had gone back to school again, as a teacher probably, as it scarcely seemed likely that she would have gone as a pupil after all she had learned from Borosov.

It was not important. What was important was that Borosov had wanted a wife, and that Helene— even though little more than a child—had wanted a husband. It is a thing, he said to himself, a sacrament, which in quite a wonderful way turns a girl into a woman.

He knew that he loved Halys. And it was a warm love, there was still passion in his blood. He wanted to possess her, the slender, young-girl body, the delicate bones beneath the flesh—but even more than that, it was her love he wanted, the full, brimming cup of her heart. He wanted her to be grateful to him; he imagined her turning a look of understanding and adoration on him. And he imagined himself teaching her, instructing her, leading her through life; he saw the two of them at concerts, visiting museums, visiting—perhaps, why not?—the capitals of Europe . . .

She lay on the other side of the room, her tear-drenched face turned away from the moonlight. She lay there like another world, asleep across a gulf of time, and he longed to make the journey. It is not age which stands between us, he said to her in his mind, but the thought of death. I see it before me and you do not. Grant me a little of your youth to stand beside me in the face of that approaching calamity. And in turn I will give you . . .

He hesitated, and tried to think of what he had to offer her. It is not very much, he admitted: a name, a home of sorts, devotion . . . I want you to marry me, Halys, for what is left of my life. I know that you love me; and that is the only thing that matters.

Comforted, his mind made up, he fell asleep and visited once more in his dreams the Place du Tertre, the Moulin de la Galette, and the gardens of the Tuileries, in company with Helene Borosov, who wore pigtails and a hair ribbon. And in his sleep the old painter smiled, because he was as young as she. "I do not love my husband," she said, giving him a fond look, "because he is so wise, but because he is so attractive to me." They were in Vienna, drinking hot chocolate with whipped cream.

In the morning when he awoke, Halys was gone.

CHAPTER 12

"So she left you," said Jon. "Why come to me?"

It was the evening of the day after. Max had gone through many emotions that first day: surprise, then impatience, then annoyance, bewilderment, anxiety . . . That night he hardly slept at all, expecting at any moment to hear the lisp of her footsteps across the patio. At the end of the second day he went to find Jon. "Halys is gone," he said, and gave him a pitiful look, frightened and humiliated.

They stood on the Santa Monica Pier at sunset, facing west across the gray-blue water to the misty loom of the Santa Monica mountains. The mountains were sea-colored, but darker than the water. Above them the ivory-peach-flushed sky was fading into melon-green, before dimming into night. A cold wind came off the water, and Max shivered. "I thought perhaps . . ." he began; he had meant to say "perhaps she had gone to you," but he couldn't get himself to say it. "I thought perhaps you might know something," he finished weakly.

"What should I know?" asked Jon harshly. "She wasn't my girl, she was yours."

"I wanted to marry her," said Max. "I was going to ask her; but then she left. . . ."

"Didn't you ask her?"

Max shook his head. "She was gone," he said. "When I woke up, she was gone."

He thought that Jon was looking at him

strangely. "She must have crept out," Max said. "I didn't even know it. But why?" he asked. "Why?"

Jon stared moodily into the slate-gray water beneath them. "I thought she was going to marry you," he said. "She said she wanted to."

"Then she knew!" exclaimed Max. "Even before I did. I can't understand it."

"Maybe she changed her mind," said Jon. So the old man was alone again, he thought; it would have made so much difference a week ago, and now it didn't matter any more. The thing was, what had happened? and where was Halys? "She wasn't any good," he said evenly, and believed it. "Just a drifter."

"That isn't true," said Max.

"She was using you," said Jon. He hated Max's loyalty; he felt a savage happiness in twisting the knife in the old man's heart. But the next moment he felt sorry for him. "After all," he said more gently, "you asked for it."

"No," said Max; "she left the dress I bought her.

She didn't take anything. She wasn't using me . . . not that way, not the way you mean. Maybe the way a bird would use the branch of a tree, to stop off and rest. But I thought I knew her. I thought . . . I thought she was happy."

"I guess that's the trouble," said Jon. "You think you know how everybody feels. Well, maybe people don't feel the same as they used to . . . when . . ."

"When I was young?" asked Max flatly.

"Well, yes," said Jon. "Like that. Maybe she just wanted out."

So, she just "wanted out," thought Max. And she had known what he was going to ask her; and rather than have to say no . . . But what sense did it make? She could have stayed on, even if . . . Of course, it wouldn't have been too easy for her, or for him, either. But to run away like that—as though he were some sort of ogre?

Perhaps Jon was right; perhaps he didn't know how people felt—young people, that is, the ones with the closed faces. They had their own way of talking, too; he knew they heard something, saw something, that he didn't see or hear; like cats, perhaps, or lunar moths. The crazy music, the high, wild, bleating, forlorn, desperate notes, the poems that made no sense, the nightmare paintings . . . *somebody saw something.* . . .

Maybe the witches were coming back. Maybe it was getting time for Hieronymus Bosch again.

But that didn't find Halys for him. "So you don't know where she is," he repeated, as though he found it hard to believe.

Jon's face remained closed and secretive. "Why don't you leave her alone?" he asked.

The old painter regarded him thoughtfully. He hates me, he thought, in spite of everything. He has no friendship for me, he does not even know who I am. Probably he never did. There is too great a gulf between the generations after all; it is too far from me to him and back again.

How could he answer him? How tell him what Halys had meant to him—how describe his hopes? (How absurd, how fantastic they seemed to him now!) How could this boy, this child, know what it was like to be offered a last handful of youth's golden dust—only to have it swept out of his grasp as he reached for it? The golden pollen . . . Did the young men and girls dust the world with it any more? How could they? We had a joy, he thought, there was a joyousness about us; but not today, for the young.

He turned and walked away. I would not want to be so hard and secret and closed, he said. I would not want to live such a bare life, without furniture.

Jon looked after him angrily. He saw a sagging body from which the sweetness and the freshness had long ago departed; the thought of that body having anything to do with Halys disgusted him. He hated to see a man make himself ridiculous; all an old man had was his dignity, his place in life; when he lost that, he lost all.

Meanwhile—where was Halys? The fact that she had left Max was like a lamp suddenly turned on inside him. He felt light and clear, took deep breaths, and smiled vaguely at passers-by. But in the very next instant he was plunged into the most frightful anxiety: suppose he couldn't find her? Suppose she had really gone off somewhere, not to be seen again? The world suddenly appeared enormous to him, very wide, and full of hiding places. Even the city was a rat's nest, a jungle, a labyrinth; even the beaches . . .

The beaches! Of course! Why hadn't he thought of it? It was just a chance, of course—and yet—he had a feeling; something told him, he was almost sure . . .

He thumbed a ride on an old truck filled with split eucalyptus logs for firewood. As long as he lived he'd remember that smell of the eucalyptus, and the ocean smell, the wet sand and the kelp, and later at the beach the smoky odor of the fires.

He found her in the dark against the cliff where they had sat before, under the black shadow of the ledge. "I wondered if you'd come," she said.

He couldn't think of anything to say; he put his arms around her, and she clung to him with all her might. "Don't let me go," she whispered. "Hold me!"

She had her old dress on, and her raincoat; as Max had said, she'd left everything else behind. They sat side by side on the cold sand, and held each other's hands. "It's crazy," he said. "The whole thing's crazy."

"Yes," she said. "I know it is." Her voice wavered a little. "I was afraid maybe you wouldn't remember this place," she said.

"It came to me all of a sudden," Jon told her. "I thought of the beach, and how we'd sat here . . ."

"You kissed me," she said. "I guess I wasn't very nice about it. I was so surprised."

"I thought you didn't like me," he said. "I thought you were mad at me, or something."

"No," she said, "I wasn't mad at you. It wasn't ever my not liking you. It was you, not liking me."

They were both silent, amazed at life's richness, confused by its complexities. "But," he said, worried, "what made you? I mean—the whole thing? Staying there with him in the first place. And then

. . . When did you know you . . . liked me?"

She bent her head, it was her turn to rake the cold sand with nervous fingers. "Last night," she said. "During the music. And then afterwards. When I knew he was going to ask me to . . . you know."

"But he didn't, did he?" asked Jon.

"No; but I knew. You know, how sometimes you get a feeling . . . And all of a sudden the thought of it . . . I knew that wasn't what I wanted at all! It made me feel so sad. And then I knew—sort of."

Her voice all but fluttered out in the night. It seemed as though she grew more and more shy, the more she spoke.

"When I woke up," she said presently, "it was early, the sun was just coming up. The whole world looked so young, and I thought: it's Jon. I mean . . . the way I felt . . . you know? All the time I was listening to the music, and then afterwards. It wasn't Max; it was you. Only I didn't know it.

"I couldn't tell him," she said; "I couldn't bear to tell him. So then I ran away, and came here."

"That was crazy," he said. "You could have come and told me."

She shivered a little. "I was scared," she said. "I didn't know how you felt; I thought if you wanted me you'd find me."

"Suppose I hadn't remembered this place?" he said. "I wouldn't ever have found you."

She shook her head helplessly. "I thought maybe you'd remember," she said, "if you cared. And if you didn't . . . I was as well off here. Anyway, I couldn't go back."

"No," he said. "No, you couldn't."

"So now," she said, "I don't know what to do."

"You're coming home with me," he declared simply. But she shook her head. "What do you mean, no?" he demanded. "I've got a place, haven't I?"

"It isn't that," she said unhappily, afraid he might think his place not good enough for her. "Please, it isn't that at all."

"Well," he said, awkwardly, "if you could go home with him . . ."

"Don't you see?" she said. "I didn't . . . like

him. Not the way I like you. It wouldn't be the same."

"All right," he said flatly, "so it wouldn't." He put his arm around her, and she leaned toward him and rested her head in a tired way against his shoulder.

"I couldn't," she said. "Not now. Not the way I feel. It was all right when I didn't care. I guess he was sort of like a father. . . . He never saw me undressed, or anything. I mean, I used to go behind the screen . . ."

"I don't want to hear about it," said Jon.

She raised her face blindly to his and their mouths met in a long kiss. "I love you," she said. "I don't ever want to hurt you."

It was the most beautiful thing he had ever heard. A sudden almost incredible joy rose like a rocket in him, filled him with light like a Roman candle. He thought he had never heard such a beautiful voice, that there had never been such tenderness in the world, or such happiness, or such a night. "I love you, too," he said, and felt his throat choke up. "Look," he said. "You don't want to stay here."

She sighed, and moved closer in his arms. "I'm hungry," she said.

He bent and kissed her eyes. "I've got some money," he declared. "If we could get to a place somewhere, I could get you something."

"All right," she said.

Half a mile down the highway they picked up a ride as far as Ocean Park, and found a small restaurant at Main and Harbor, and went in and sat down in a booth, facing each other. She looked tired; her hair was loose over her shoulders, and she leaned her head wearily on her hand. "I'm beat," she said, and smiled mournfully at him across the table.

He leaned forward and took her elbow in his hand. It was so light and small. . . . "I'm going to take care of you," he announced; "from now on."

"Yes," she said. Why not? she thought; he was a caterpillar, but so was she. She was tired of getting out from under people's feet. "I'll take care of you, too," she said. "Someday, when I feel better."

He ordered her a beef stew; she picked at it mincingly at first, but after a while she was eating it hungrily, and sopping up the gravy with a piece of bread. While she ate, he watched her, his face full of wonder and joy. "Tell me," he said: "tell me how you knew. Was it because of that night when I kissed you and you acted so scared?"

"Maybe," she said; "I don't know. I think it was before that, but I don't know. Maybe it was from the very beginning."

"Me too," he said happily. "I was mad at you for coming between us. Max and me, that is. Anyway, I thought that was it. I guess what I was mad at was your staying there in his room with him."

"You were jealous," said Halys simply.

"Yes; I guess I was."

"I didn't know," she said. "He was so nice to me; and you didn't come around, and you wouldn't talk to me. So then, after the concert, I kissed him; and all the time I was thinking, if only it was different . . ." She glanced up at him shyly. "I guess I knew at the beach that night," she said, "that I didn't want anybody to . . . well . . . to ever kiss me like that, except you."

"That's when I knew it, too," said Jon.

"So then," she said, "when I thought about how it would be . . . well, you know . . . marrying him, and everything . . . I suddenly got this feeling like I was saying good-by to something."

They smiled at each other across the table top. They were still amazed, still not quite able to believe what had happened, to understand that they had found each other, after all. Jon saw Halys as though he had never really seen her before; she was like a succession of strangers, each one alluring, troubling in a different way, suddenly beautiful, suddenly touching; the love in her eyes as she looked at him was something he could almost feel, like the warmth of a fire, it was almost a substance. It filled him with longing, with unbearable happiness. "It'll be different now," he said.

To Max, too, it would be different. He sat alone

in his studio waiting for Halys to come back and knowing that she wouldn't. It was not so much the girl herself he mourned; what gave him anguish was the sense of something lost—something gone irrevocably from his life, a period, a time of himself that would never come again.

CHAPTER 13

Jon and Halys were married in Mexico the next day. They took the morning bus to Tijuana and returned the same evening; it was a long, hot ride, and the little bouquet of flowers she carried was wilted by the time she got back to Santa Monica. She put the flowers in the washbowl in Jon's room, and took off her raincoat and hung it in the closet. She had nothing else to put there.

She sat down on the bed, and looked around her. Was she really married? All she felt was confused and a little sad. This was her home now; when she got a job, they'd put up some curtains and buy a lamp and a comfortable chair. Only, first she'd have to get some clothes; she couldn't be married and have only one dress, and no nightgown. She wished she had a pretty nightgown to wear for Jon to see her in. She wondered where the bathroom was; it embarrassed her to have to ask.

They were still shy with each other, not knowing what to say, feeling a little frightened because they didn't feel happier. "I think they probably knew we were married," said Jon; "those people on the bus."

"I guess they probably did," said Halys.

"On account of your carrying flowers, and everything," said Jon.

"They were pretty flowers," said Halys.

"Would you like something to eat?" he asked. "I could go out and get something."

"I'm not hungry," she said.

"I guess you must be pretty tired," he said; "it was kind of a long ride there and back."

"Yes," she said; "and the heat."

"It was hot, all right," he said.

But after a while there was nothing more to say, and nothing to do but go to bed. And then, in the dark, suddenly, it all grew mysterious again, and warm and secret; the night, and the two of them close, and Halys's hair fragrant on the pillow and her breath sweet, and all in whispers, hidden from the world, belonging only to each other, belonging together forever and ever . . .

They slept at last, exhausted, and with a sense of wonder at God's amazing thoughtfulness and generosity. "I had no idea," said Halys humbly; it was, in its way, a prayer of thanks.

The dawn wind, mysterious and lonely, blew inland from the sea, and Halys awoke to a new world, not knowing for a moment where she was. Jon lay asleep beside her, his head pillowed on his hand. She stared at him drowsily, in sleepy surprise to see him look so young, so innocent and stern;

what was going on behind those closed eyes? in that shut and secret brain? Was he happy? pleased with her? Would he be glad that they were married? Was he dreaming, even now? Was it light there, merry or sad? or was it all dark and empty like the space between the worlds? She closed her eyes for a moment, and fell back on the pillow. Now she, too, had shut the door on the world; it drifted away from her like smoke, a blur of faint sensation, vague memories . . .

When she opened her eyes again, Jon was standing there already dressed, drinking from a cup and munching a piece of bread. "I made the coffee," he said. "I didn't want to wake you up." He bent uncertainly to kiss her; she drew the sheets up around her nakedness, and then put her arms around his neck. "Yes," she said.

"It's late," he told her. "I've got to go. I'll bring back something for lunch."

Left to herself, she washed and dressed, and got herself some breakfast of cornflakes and milk, coffee and bread. Jon had no icebox, he kept things like milk and butter outdoors, on the windowsill. The flowers from yesterday were quite dead, they hadn't revived over night. She took the little bouquet out of the washbowl, and dried it off and put it in the closet with her raincoat. She had no wedding ring, they had had to borrow one from the official in Tijuana—the judge, or whatever he was. Jon had said he'd get her a ring later; she couldn't help wondering if he'd have money enough. Not that it mattered really, she thought, but it would be nice to have a wedding ring.

For the rest of the morning she sat on the bed, or wandered dreamily around the room, looking at Jon's few belongings . . . hers, too, now. He had so little: two cups (one with the handle broken off), three plates (two of them were chipped), two knives, but only one fork, three spoons, an old coffee pot for boiling water, and a frying pan. He had almost as few clothes as she had. She found a rusty toilet down the hall, but she had no idea where the bathtub was—or if there was one. Like

Max, Jon had a gas ring to cook on, but no screen between the bed and the washbasin. There was so much he needed—they needed! I'm going to have to get a job, she thought; I'm going to have to. I want us to have a home.

She found a photograph of Jon's family in the top of a cheap chest of drawers; some older people and younger ones seated in front of what she guessed was probably the farm in Oklahoma. Jon was there, too; he must have been about twelve years old at the time. She couldn't tell who anybody was, but they all looked like nice people. Solid people, who worked hard and didn't smile much. The two older ones must be his father and mother. She wondered what they thought of having a painter for a son; she wondered what they'd think of her.

She found Jon's canvases stacked against the wall, and pulled them out to look at. She didn't know anything about painting—only what Max had told her—but she liked them. The colors were so . . . so what? She didn't know exactly, but it was as if everything was in bright air. The thing was, there weren't any people in the pictures, only places. When Jon painted a street, he left it empty, there wasn't anybody walking on it or going anywhere. But always somewhere in the painting there was a faraway point, and everything led to it.

That was something Max had told her about. She supposed she ought to think of him as Mr. Loeb now.

Jon came back at noon with a fresh loaf of bread, a wedge of processed cheese, two slices of ham, and a pickle. They ate their lunch seated on the bed side by side, and smoked a cigarette, leaning back against the pillow. "Is it all right?" he asked. "You aren't sorry, or anything?"

"No," she said. "Are you?"

He seemed reassured. "I was wondering if you were really here," he said.

"When I woke up," she admitted, "I didn't know where I was for a minute."

"As long as you're happy," he said; "the way I am."

"It's a funny thing. When you're with me, I'm so happy I can hardly stand it."

"I know. I'm the same way."

She locked her fingers tightly in his, and leaned her head against his shoulder. "Do you ever feel like you were in church?" she asked; "sort of?"

"Yes," he said. "That's how I feel."

Once again they turned to each other, timidly at first, and then with longing as the whole sea of love rose over them.

They were young, passionate, and innocent. It was enough for them; it was enough that they were the way they were.

When it was time for Jon to go back to the market, he kissed Halys's closed and shadowed eyes. For a while she slept, and then she drowsed. She thought vaguely that she ought to sweep, or dust, or learn something about how to cook, but she felt too comfortable, it was too delicious lying there and dreaming.

So this was love; and this was marriage. Not only last night, but now.

She stretched out lazily in the bed—and thought suddenly, for no good reason, of Max, and turned hot with embarrassment. Now that she knew . . . she never could have made love with Max. She never could have; never!

And Max, going about his daily business, buying his food—but at a different market to avoid seeing Jon; working—but without diligence or enthusiasm —on his beach picture, or walking under the trees along Ocean Avenue, in the shaded park with the sea below, asked himself what it was like to be jilted in such a fashion and by such a girl.

He had no easy answer to give himself. He had wanted to believe something . . . and he had believed it. For a while, anyway. The Lord giveth, he told himself wryly, and the Lord taketh away. It all comes from somewhere, he said, the good and the bad.

He knew that Jon and Halys were married, because Jon had written him a letter about it. It wasn't much of a letter: only "Dear Mr. Max Loeb, we are married and everything is all right." And signed "Sincerely yours."

What bothered him was the fact that he didn't feel as wretched as he thought he ought to. There was no doubt that he was unhappy—humiliated, ashamed, and lonely. On the other hand, he knew that he was glad to be alone at such a time; he valued his loneliness, there was something comforting about it. He liked being his own, only friend; and there was no possibility of his being misunderstood.

After all, what had happened? He had taken a young girl to live with him, sheltered her, bought her a dress, and fallen in love with her. He had allowed himself to imagine, to dream . . . And she had left him for a younger man. That was the kind of thing that happened every day, he supposed, to somebody; why shouldn't it have happened to him? And as he walked, he repeated to himself, more or less musically, Tristan's answer to King Mark's question: *"Oh,* König, *das kann ich dir nicht sagen!* I do not know, I cannot tell you."

In other words, he had been like other foolish old men.

And yet, he thought, she did love me; what I took for love was true and real. I should have realized that there are many grades of love, like eggs, or butter. What a mother feels for her daughter, or a father for his son, are different and yet the same; but what an old man feels for a young woman, or a young woman feels for a young man, are not the same at all. And what Halys felt for me was still different; those rockets in the blood, those pinwheels and Roman candles I remember from my youth made no uproar in her breast.

Still, if I am honest . . . did they in mine? Is it possible that I no longer feel that passionate absorption of the mind, that exaltation of the senses which, combined with jealousy, a nervous stomach, and the expectation of setting the world on fire, informed my earlier years?

He burst out laughing at himself. I am thinking in the style of some writer of the nineteenth century, he said. Well, the devil with it!

But it wasn't as easily settled as all that. There was still to be faced the panic-sense of time—the realization that time was growing shorter, and the deadline nearer. Time for what? and what deadline? He didn't know: was it to have a success? or find happiness? or love? He had had all three—though not, he had to admit, so much of the first.

What was it, then, he had to find? Grow old along with me, he thought: what nonsense! Things only get worse, never better. And yet he had no desire to be young again. It is a mistake, he said to himself, to think of youth as a happy time. It is an intense time—and ankle-deep in suffering. All the answers for which the young man waits are still ahead of him. The trouble is that for me, too, at this moment they are still ahead, and no closer.

Once more he examined the thought of that moment when he would have to make up his mind, would have to know . . . what? Some truth, he thought, some answer: what Hermione knew when she knelt in prayer; what Jon knows, he thought, when he sinks on Halys's breast . . . and then forgets again. Something about life, and God, and eternity . . .

I will be very frightened when I come to die, he thought, if I have not found that answer.

In the midst of these reflections he was struck with a sudden feeling of anguish. I am less attractive to myself now, he remarked, since I have been proven so unattractive to Halys. But the next moment he scolded himself for self-pity. At least, he declared, I am no worse off than I was a month ago.

Not that age was entirely without its compensations. There was the sweetness of sleep, the stealing away . . . And twilight came down without stirring a sorrow in the heart, and there was nothing to run home to, there was time, plenty of time, no need to hurry . . . But Oh, he cried out silently, I was young for a little while!

At least, he added a moment later, I felt young.

CHAPTER 14

Now that Jon had Halys, he could hardly wait to do her portrait. It was as if, with the original in front of him, he wanted to make his own extra copy, in case the other should ever be lost. Or perhaps it was to get down on canvas something that only he saw—some look, some glimpse of beauty, of joy or innocence apparent only to himself.

He set to work feverishly, painting in the early

morning and again in the evening before supper to catch what light was left. It was scarcely an ideal arrangement, but it was the best he could do, and still hold down his job at the market. And Halys was pleased, though it made a long day for her; and in the morning sometimes she went back to sleep again after Jon left. She was still trying to make up for all the many sleepless days and nights in the past. Then, later, when she'd swept, and made the bed, and done the dishes, she'd go down to the beach at the end of the street, to lie in the sun for a while, or dabble her feet in the water. Someday, when she had a job, she'd get herself a bathing suit.

Sometimes Jon brought milk and cheese and crackers to the beach, or free samples from the market, and they ate their lunch together sitting on the sand; but most of the time she met him back in the room where it was shadowy and where it was still faintly cool from the night before. In the evening, when she had finished posing for him, they walked together hand in hand in the dim blue air through the yellow-lighted streets, stopping somewhere for coffee and pie, or going home with a can of spaghetti from the market, or half a pound of hamburger. Or they went to Ocean Park and stood outside the gates and listened to the music from the merry-go-round and the sky-rides, and looked at the lights and the people, and bought spun sugar to eat, and felt extravagant and rich.

She liked Jon's portrait better than the picture Max had painted of her sitting in front of the fire. That figure had been so sad—so weary and lost, with the night all around it, and other people's fires. The face that looked out of Jon's canvas was a bright, daytime face, with small, clean bones under the flesh; it was the face he saw, loving her, and it was what she wanted him to see. "I think you're a better painter than Max," she said. "I really do."

He didn't know whether to be pleased or not. He wanted her to say things like that; and yet, she knew so little! "Oh, well," he said; "maybe some-day . . ."

"If I could only be a help to you," she said. "If only I could help."

"You do," he assured her. "You do help."

They were happy, but they were poor—too poor, in fact, even for people like themselves who had never been anything else. And as the days went by, Halys began to think more and more about looking for work. She wished she could make a lot of money—enough to pay the rent on a better place, to buy herself some clothes, but most of all to make it possible for Jon to give up his job and devote all his time to his painting. It was a new experience for her, but she had never expected to be an artist's wife. "When I think how hard it is for you," she told him, "and with a wife besides . . . You're too good a painter to have to work daytimes in a market."

When he stopped to consider it, he was inclined to agree with her. "Maybe you're right," he said. "Maybe if you had a job . . ."

She had expected him to love her for it, and couldn't understand why she felt suddenly so depressed. "You mean you wouldn't mind?" she asked in a puzzled way.

He looked at her in surprise. Why should he mind? He was happy to think that she loved him that much. Where he came from, women worked anyway, the same as men. "No," he said. "Why should I?"

"Well," she said slowly, "I wouldn't be around during the day."

Yet she herself had made the offer—out of a need to be loved, to be useful to him, needing to be wanted . . . Most men wouldn't care to have their wives support them. She'd be out, working, while he stayed home.

She felt very sorry for herself. "We wouldn't have lunch together any more," she said, thinking about it. "And I wouldn't be able to pose for you."

Jon experienced a sudden feeling of impatience. After all, he hadn't asked her to, so why did she say she wanted to if she didn't want to? "Let's leave things the way they are," he said shortly. "We're getting along all right."

But that was even worse, she thought, for him to see so little the way it really was. "We're not getting along," she said. "I haven't even got a nightgown."

"What difference does it make?" said Jon. He needed a few things, too: fresh tubes of ochre and burnt sienna, a fine brush, another stretcher for his canvas . . .

She was used to going without; it was only that she'd have felt more married if she could have gone to bed in a nightgown, she'd have felt different. And she wanted to feel different . . . the way she'd felt in the garage—the studio, that was— with Max . . . with Mr. Loeb. When she'd had all those things: the pajamas and the old bathrobe and the dress from Mrs. Bloemendal . . . Not, of course, that she missed them, or that she wanted to be like that again. But it would have been nice to have a nightgown. She would have felt more dignified, more like a wife . . . cherished.

Two nights later Halys got a job baby-sitting for the owner of the market. She and Jon sat together in front of Mr. Herndon's television set, along with the two Herndon children, and the four of them watched a horror show, three shootings (Western style), two crime shows (Eastern type), and a quiz. Gorged on this feast of spirit, and on graham crackers and milk, the children went off to bed at midnight, convinced that in a world where might so obviously made right, the only sensible thing was to grow up as rapidly as possible, and beat people's brains out. Their parents, returning an hour later, paid Halys three dollars and fifty cents, which seemed to her almost a fortune.

"Why," she said to Jon on their way home, "if I could make that much every night . . ."

Jon sighed and yawned. "It makes a long day," he said. "For me, anyway."

She took his arm, and rubbed her cheek against the rough cotton of his sleeve. "I know," she said. "It's the only time we have together. I don't want to spend it in other people's houses."

"Looking at a lot of . . ." said Jon.

"Don't say it," she said. "It was a lovely evening."

Three dollars and fifty cents. She could get a nightgown, a bathing suit, panties, a dress . . . She thought of all the things she needed, and her spirits sank. She'd have to make a choice: one thing only, and not the most expensive, either. What would it be? Some dishes? A pot for the stove? A sweater? A scarf for her hair?

The next morning, after Jon had left for work, Halys went quietly into Santa Monica and bought him a near-leather wallet with his initials on it in gold. She gave it to him that night, and after he had thanked her, he put everything he had into it: two one-dollar bills, his social-security card, a small snapshot of his family, and an Oklahoma junior driver's license which had expired several years before. Then he folded the wallet, and put it in his back pocket, and took it out again, and looked at it. "That's wonderful," he said. "That's really wonderful."

"I wanted you to have it," said Halys. "I wanted to give you something you'd like."

Touched and proud, he stooped to her.

"I'm going to be the best wife," she said: "the best in the whole world."

"Sure," he said. "You are, anyway."

He really thought so; and he continued to think so even when Halys, meaning to surprise him one evening with supper already cooked and waiting, dropped the whole pan of corned-beef hash mixed with green peppers and chopped onions onto the floor, and, after standing a moment in silent horror, walked out, quietly weeping, from failure, and from the onions, leaving the mess for Jon when he got home, to eat if he liked, or to throw out, and to forgive her if possible.

He forgave her, they had cornflakes and milk, and went to bed, where, curled up against his back, she sang in a small, sad, tuneless voice: "I'll take you home again, Kathleen." It was one of the two songs she knew; the other was "I'm tying the leaves so they won't fall down." They were songs her grandmother sang to her when she was a little girl—long ago, she thought; long, long ago.

It made her homesick, though she didn't know for what; she'd never had a home to be homesick for. Except, maybe, for those weeks with Max— with Mr. Loeb; but that was over now. She was married, and in love with her husband.

Still, there were times when they didn't seem to have very much to say to each other. Once or twice she tried to talk to Jon about his painting, but it wasn't anything he wanted to talk about. Not with her, anyway; she didn't know enough. He needed to talk to somebody who did.

He was beginning to feel uncertain; after the first rush of energy and enthusiasm, his painting disappointed him; it wasn't as good as he'd thought. There was so much that he didn't know how to do yet. . . . He grew impatient with himself. The room seemed smaller, too, with both of them in it all the time. . . . Well, that was to be expected. But sometimes he had a feeling that the walls were closing in on him; his whole life seemed to be closing in, the far-off, airy, wide horizons were narrowing down, growing tighter. . . . He wanted to take deep breaths, run, fling his arms around, cry out; he wanted to be great, he wanted to be happy and to be great.

If it wasn't going to be like that, what was the good of being Jon Kuzik?

Nothing was working out the way they had expected; not the way people wrote about it. They were in love, and they were together, and that ought to have been everything, and enough; but somehow—and sometimes—it wasn't. Moments of excitement and happiness had a way of ebbing away, leaving a sadness, almost a loneliness . . . and Jon would turn in on himself, and Halys would feel unwanted and in the way. And she would wonder what good she was to him; and from there it wasn't a long step to thinking about herself, and what future did she have?

There were even times now and then—on a hot, dusty day—when they would look at each other as though they were strangers, with sudden fright;

what were they doing together, there in that small, poor room, which smelled of paint, and cooking, and Halys's cheap perfume? Then, at such moments, they wanted desperately to reach out to one another, to talk to each other, about life, about love, about themselves, about anything . . . but they had so little to talk about. They had so little to help them, their hold on joy was spider-thin.

Jon had stopped working on Halys's portrait, and had put it away; he didn't seem to have any interest in it any more. He was working on something else; whatever it was, he turned it carefully to the wall when he went off in the morning. It was as though he didn't want her to see it; as though he didn't want to talk about it. She turned it around one day, and looked at it for a long time. It was a street, ending in a wall: an empty street, with no one on it.

Meanwhile, back at Mrs. Bloemendal's, Hermione was busily sewing up a tear in one of Mr. Loeb's shirts. She had nearly lost her tenant, she had had a narrow escape, and she knew that when a man's pride shattered—or even if only his vanity was cracked—the best thing for a woman to do was to mend something.

Mr. Loeb was not too unhappy, though still a little shaken by what had happened. He was enjoying, for the moment, a small success in the world of art: another painting had been sold through that same dealer who had sold his earlier picture of the Malibu hills, and his charcoal studies of Halys were being shown at a gallery in Long Beach. He no longer wanted to keep them for himself; he did not feel that he could afford to; unlike other mementos—the review from *The New York Times,* a silk garter, a program from the Bal Tabarin, a toothpick from Polly's in Greenwich Village—they were not souvenirs of a success. His portrait of the retired chiropractor was going to earn him a substantial fee; it was not yet begun, but he had accepted a small advance; and his speech to the ladies of the Julia A. Moore Club had been a great success. "No poets in the past," he had said to them in discussing the poets of the present, "ever spent so much time trying to say so little to so few."

He had also discussed such things as styles in women's dresses. "Men," he said, "have been reduced little by little to simplicity, redesigned, as it were, in the sole interest of function. They have moved from the rich fashion of the Renaissance through the dignified dress of the Victorians to our own rude and slovenly attire—always away from fashion, and toward use and action; while woman still arranges and rearranges her clothing in the brightest of colors, one way this year, the next year another way, now long, now short, now loose, now tight, but always dainty, extravagant, and formidable; and thus maintains her dominion over the male, since she not only bears his child, but wears his plumage."

In closing, he had this to say about modern art —of the modern primitives he said: "We have had primitives before during the Dark Ages; they were innocent and naïve; they painted as they did because they didn't know any better. Today's primitives also paint in a naïve style, but they are not so innocent. Perhaps we are going into another Dark Ages."

Of the abstractionists he had this to say: "We are no longer expected to see with our eyes what another man has seen with his—but to take in, to ingest, as it were, in one swallow, by a convulsion of the imagination, what he has felt while brooding upon some obscure thought.

"Well, that is very hard to explain, how to look at a thought: one can only look at it with another thought. So now it is possible for a picture to mean one thing to the man who painted it, and quite another to the man who is looking at it.

"This does not seem in any way to spoil the value of such paintings, which bring higher and higher prices every day."

Coming home, still remembering the taste of the tea and the little cakes he had eaten, he said to Mrs. Bloemendal, his companion: "How was I?"

"Well," said Hermione, "I think they liked you. I don't think they understood you very well."

Mr. Loeb drove along in silence for a while. Then he exclaimed in decisive tones: "We have the greatest mass production of mediocrity the world has ever seen. Everything is aimed at the lowest common denominator. Did *you* understand me?"

"Of course," said Hermione, crossing her fingers.

She meant that she was proud of him, and a little surprised, the way a mother is proud and surprised to hear her son deliver the Latin oration at his graduation; and she felt sorry for him because of Halys, and because his clothes were old and worn, and now that she stopped to think about it, slovenly.

CHAPTER 15

THE old painter lay in his bed, gravely ill. That is
to say, he was suffering from influenza and a bron-
chial affection, but no one felt alarmed about it
except himself. When he woke at night, wet with
perspiration, aching, and with leaden limbs, he
thought of all the disasters which could end a

man's life, and he groaned aloud. In the darkness, which seemed to him alive and like a moving cloud, he felt that he was suffocating with fright; he felt unable to reason or to think about anything, he felt that he was a rat in a trap, and that there was nothing to do but accept his fate and wait. However, in the morning he usually felt better, and then he was able to reflect on man's life and on his own.

What a frail creature man was, after all! It took so little to lay him flat, to squash him like a beetle under somebody's heel. And then he was dead . . . along with all the countless billions since Paleolithic man . . . all his fathers and his great-grandfathers . . .

If only he knew what death was like. Was there a last dream, and no waking up from it? only a dimming, a vanishing of the light? only emptiness, nothingness, the dark? Yet, emptiness and darkness were abstractions, they were words, thoughts . . . There was no such thing as darkness, actually, except to eyes accustomed to the light. When God said "Let there be light," where was He speaking from?

Left field, perhaps?

There it was again—that matter of God: and Max Loeb had no picture of Him in his mind at all. Or perhaps he had too many. There was His picture as the head of a school, the president of a country club, the father of a family; but who was captain of the asteroids? And was there ever a time before God was? and when was that? and what was that? and what was in it? And did God enclose space—or did space enclose Him? And in what relation was a drop of water to the cosmos?

It is useless, he thought; we cannot think these things out, not even along the lines of an expanding universe, or a vast explosion. We must simply jump like a grasshopper into the infinite, with nothing but faith to propel us. And here is the very core of my problem, because when I say faith, I must ask myself: Faith in what? and I do not have any answer. I might say: Faith in what is; but something is missing, it doesn't sustain me. I do not wish to be counted in with the mosquito, the man-eating shark, the pneumococcus, and the rat; I demand something nobler for myself than kinship with the worm, or to be blood brother to the spirochete. I long to believe in a felicity, a continuing good for mankind, because I am a man, and not a sea anemone, or a rabbit. I envy Hermione, who believes that after death her soul is going somewhere; what frightens me is the thought that mine is not going anywhere at all, not even in some vast stream flowing between the stars, and in which I would be happy to have a part as insignificant but as personal as a herring.

"Here," said Hermione, coming into the studio with a tray, "is your chicken broth."

Mr. Loeb sat up in bed to eat his supper. The light was fading, and he tried to think of something to say, some way to keep Mrs. Bloemendal with him a little longer. At the same time he realized that he did not present a very attractive appearance, with an unshaven bristle on his chin, his hair rumpled, and his bedclothes untidy. It was not the sort of thing to rouse a woman's admiration, or give her a feeling of security.

"You look better," said Hermione. "Your color isn't so bad."

"I am very uncomfortable," said Mr. Loeb. He was seized with a sudden enormous pity for himself, lying there disheveled and uneasy, while this erect, blooming, hearty woman moved in such a free and healthy way around the room. It seemed to him that he had never really seen her before. And, looking up at her, with the tray on his lap, he thought: She is kinder than I imagined.

He considered the element of kindness, and how it gave dignity to a face, and even a sort of beauty. A woman like that, he thought, does not need any security from me, she has her own. Still, I wish I looked a little more appetizing. I do not like to be an object of pity for other people; for myself, of course, that's another matter.

And in mournful tones he exclaimed: "You are being good to an old man."

Mrs. Bloemendal gave him a bright smile, and patted his feet under the covers. "Don't talk like that," she said. "You're not an old man yet, by a long shot. And anyway," she added, "when a woman can't cook a little chicken broth for a friend . . . After all—we've known each other a long while."

Max lay back dizzily on his pillow. He could have wept, from loneliness, and out of gratitude for a woman's kindness. Yes, he thought, we have known each other a long while . . . but we have never really spoken before. There is somebody here who is both a stranger and a friend; and I do not even know what she looks like. . . .

Hermione was gazing at the painting of the beach, at the figure of Halys in front of the fire. And suddenly, as though she could see everything through Max's eyes, she understood the whole sad little love affair. And in gentle tones she inquired: "Would you like me to rub your back for you?"

"Yes," said Mr. Loeb. "I would."

Under her soft yet strong fingers, the muscles

slowly unknotted themselves, and Mr. Loeb began to feel comfortable, and even a little sleepy. There was something about it which reminded him of the past, when other fingers had soothed him—his mother's at first, and later the hands of other women. . . . He had had no reason to be ashamed of his body in those days; it was youthful and strong, and they had found it not unattractive. He felt warm and drowsy; his landlady's hands felt gentle and firm on his back. . . . It was like long ago. Other mornings, other years, other evenings . . .

Hermione, too, was aware of something. For one thing, the skin she was kneading was so soft . . . like velvet, she thought. Perhaps he wasn't so old, after all—or perhaps she didn't know what being old was. . . . A kind of heat seemed to rise from his flesh through her fingers to her heart and her face; she couldn't help the thoughts that came to her, the misty images that formed in her mind and then immediately dissolved again. Holy Mother, she thought in dismay, what's going on here? She closed her eyes for a moment. It's the temperature, she told herself; God help me, it's the sickness in him that's maybe catching.

"That's enough of that," she said aloud, giving him a wholesome slap on the shoulder. "Hold still, now, while I put the talcum on you."

He lay quiet, drifting off into sleep, sunk in drowsy acceptance, while a phrase repeated itself over and over in his mind—something he had heard, or was it something he had said? He didn't know, and it didn't matter. A woman's hands, he thought, they express everything. And then he thought: All this is no accident.

Turning his head a little, he half glanced up at her where her figure rose tall and shadowy beside his bed. "What have the galaxies got to do with it?" he asked. "Tell me that."

"Indeed," she said, "I wouldn't know."

"Then I'll tell you," he said. "There was never anything in creation was meant to be alone."

"I know that," she said, troubled. "But between what was meant, and the way it is . . ."

"It would be nice to have someone here," said Max, "to keep the night frights away."

"I've often thought the same," said Hermione; "even to hear a snore now and then is a comfort." Her throat felt a little thick, and she seemed to be having difficulty with her speech. It's the sickness, she thought; I've caught it off him.

Even so, she was surprised at her own boldness; it seemed such a delicate thing to discuss, the way her husband used to snore. She felt flushed with embarrassment, and with something more, a feeling of excitement or at least suspense, as though there might be something hiding in the shadows —something a little frightening, a danger, though she couldn't see what there was to be afraid of if she sat for a while out of Christian charity in the dusk of evening with a sick man . . . and him her own tenant besides.

The light deepened outside, and in the studio the shadows darkened. And Max, lying in the comfort of her nearness, saw in his mind another canvas to be painted, different from the one he had

done of Halys by the fire. It, too, was a figure—the
figure of a mature woman, bending, perhaps over
a child, with the same bowed lines of the back, but
generous this time, and full of grace, and the hands
held out as though to comfort and to accept.

Why have you sorrowed? he asked himself gently; is it for something you had? Yes, he replied,
for something long ago. Did you expect to keep it
with you forever? he asked. No, he said; but it is
a parting, and all partings are mournful, and perhaps this one most of all. How long would you have
been happy, he asked, with such a young love? I
don't know, he answered; perhaps not very long;
but how long do I have to live? not forever, either.
Did you hope to be young again yourself? No, he
said, not really; I should not like to be so grieved
again. Were you often grieved? he asked, and he
replied: Young people always are.

But they are strong, and a young girl is willowy,
and the curving, clean lines of her body are beautiful and moving. How long can a person be willowy? he thought; it isn't always spring. A man

keeps going back to the springtime of his life, not seeing the bright summer around him, the rich fall . . .

I am sentimentalizing that rich fall, he told himself wryly. It is wasp-bitten and spider-hung.

Yet, to the winter-bound voyager, it was beautiful.

CHAPTER 16

THINGS were not going well for the Kuziks. The only work that Halys had been able to find was night work—baby-sitting, waiting on table, a clean-up job at a small café. It cut into their few hours together. Once or twice Jon came home and found Halys already gone out, and when she came back, it was late and she was tired. Even their love-making wasn't quite the same; sometimes there was a note almost of anger in it, an exasperation, as though they wanted to forget something—themselves, each other, the unfurnished room, the narrow bed, the bare life around them. Afterwards they had nothing to say; they smiled at each other a little pitifully, shame-faced and embarrassed.

There was never enough money. And Jon missed the old man; he had to admit it to himself. He had a strange feeling sometimes, as though he was falling, it was like falling in an elevator, suddenly . . . a frightened, lonely, empty feeling in his stomach; and it was because Max wasn't there any more, because there was no one to turn to, no one to help him—no one but Halys. He couldn't turn to her, she couldn't help him, she didn't know any more than he did . . . all she'd do was to give him that sad little smile, as though she realized her own inadequacy.

She did her best. But for Halys the long hot days seemed to grow longer and longer; and the times of being lonely came more and more often. If only they could go somewhere—out into the cool, airy, blue, bright world, somewhere, anywhere. If only we had room to breathe, she thought, if only we had a place to live.

She wasn't being a help to him, and she knew it. It was a heavy thing in her heart; how did a person go about being a help to someone? She didn't know. She didn't even know if he needed her; not really, not any more.

She tried to remember their first days together, when it was all new and strange and like a dream. So many things had been fun . . . even to stand outside the amusement park and listen to the music. Well . . . it wasn't fun any more. Something—something merry and careless had gone out of things. Sometimes it seemed to her that she wasn't even young any more, but old and worn; she wondered if Jon saw it, too, if that was the trouble. It was as though she had been given a chance at something—something good, something wonderful

—and had missed it. But why? How had it happened? Whose fault was it? If only they could have a little fun again . . .

"Why don't you ever take me out to dinner?" she asked. "Why don't we ever do anything nice?"

He looked at her in blank astonishment. Take her out to dinner? What money did he have to take her anywhere at all? "What's the matter with where we are?" he said. "You liked it all right before."

"What I didn't think," she said, "was that we were going to stay here the rest of my life."

The rest of your life, he thought, feeling suddenly bitter, the rest of your life! You've only been here—how many weeks? six? "Look," he said, "if you don't like it . . ."

"Like it or not like it . . . I only said—"

"I know what you said. I've got ears."

"All right . . . so I said it. Don't you ever want to do anything in the world?"

"I was doing all right before you came."

[196]

"Well," she cried, "if that's the way you feel . . ."

She was hurt to the heart; and so was he. But the end was always the same: he would take hold of her by the elbows, in a sort of desperation, and after a few rebellious wrenchings and twistings, and a few mournful murmurs, they would melt into each other's arms, tearful, frantic, wet with perspiration, and contrite.

Then afterwards, for a while, they would be gentle with each other, and make vague plans. "Maybe I could find a steady job somewhere during the day," Halys would say; and Jon would talk about attending art classes at the City College, or going off to live in Mexico. But it was all just dreaming, there was no real hope behind it; dreaming and wishing, and knowing there was nothing in it. Little by little the loneliness would come down again between them; like a fog, she thought, like the fog at Playa del Rey.

And little by little, Halys found her thoughts turning back to Max. I was almost in love with him, she thought; maybe after a while I would have been. And he was in love with me; he would have married me.

Anyway, he had liked her; he had wanted her to stay. He had wanted her . . . and she had run away. She wondered if he remembered; she wondered if he had forgiven her. I didn't want to hurt you, she said to him in her mind; I didn't mean it that way. She had been happy there in the studio with him—or at least that was the way it seemed to her now, remembering. They had both been happy, hadn't they? It had been a happy time. He couldn't have forgotten that, what it had been like. He had wanted her; she had been useful to him, posing for him, and everything . . . Useful; she had been useful to him. He had needed her; she had been needed.

Jon didn't need her. There was something sad about herself and Jon, something doomed, already lost, like children in a storybook lost in a wood. That's what they were, really: children; the world was too big for them, too wide and echoing and lonely. Love was a sadness, a grief, a sorrow; they were forlorn, it was hard to remember that they had ever been anything else.

Why couldn't it have been different? Poor Jon . . .

It had all seemed so simple at first; they were young, and in love, and so they were married. They should have lived happily ever after; people always did, in stories . . . or almost always. Young people, that is, like herself and Jon; not old people, like her parents. Being married was like having your own garden, with a fence around it; or was it? There was no one to ask, no one to tell her. If Jon were alone, he could manage; if she wasn't there, being an expense to him, taking half the little he had . . . as he said, he'd got along all right before.

Oh, Jon, she thought miserably, why did it have to be like this? Why couldn't I have been everything you needed?

It was funny how lonely she felt, as if she didn't have anybody at all. When she really didn't have anybody, the way it used to be, she hadn't felt that lonely.

And all the time, there, down a few streets, not far away at all, was Max. She thought of the walks they used to take together in the evening, she and Max, the suppers out, or with Max cooking those marvelous dishes for her (or at least that was the way she remembered them), the lazy mornings, the breakfasts by the window, the cool evenings coming down, the nights with their smell of jasmine, the mockingbirds singing, a bed of her own, a screen to dress behind . . .

Oh, Jon, she cried out to him soundlessly in anguish, we don't even have a screen!

CHAPTER 17

From the window of her upstairs sitting room Hermione Bloemendal watched Halys coming down the street. "Halys is here," she remarked to Max. "I'll leave you to talk to her." But at the door she hesitated a moment. "You won't need me?" she asked uneasily, as though she wanted him to say yes, he did need her; "you'll be all right?"

What she meant was, would he still feel the same way about her after he had seen Halys? "You aren't going to be sorry?" she asked shyly.

Max smiled at her gaily. "No," he said; "I'm not going to be sorry." He was finished with all that; a man doesn't find peace, he thought, merely to lose it again. There was a certain order to life, it had form, like any other work of art. When a man knew what he wanted to paint, he didn't scrub it out in order to repeat something he'd done much earlier. Not if he had any sense. Not even Picasso would make a mistake like that. Not even Miró.

Halys had expected to find Max in the studio; but the garage doors were locked, and instead she saw Mrs. Bloemendal beckoning to her from across the patio. "I suppose you've come to see Mr. Loeb," Hermione remarked. "Well, he's upstairs."

Halys gazed at her blankly. Upstairs?—why would he be upstairs? "I wonder if I could see him for a moment," she said humbly. "I mean—if it would be convenient."

She looks terrible, thought Hermione; she looks

as if she hadn't had a good meal in weeks. Ah, well, she thought, some people go from one frying pan to another.

But she felt sorry for Halys; she didn't like her —she never had, for that matter—and when she thought of the way Halys had treated Max, how she had made use of him, and the way she'd run off and left him, without a word before or since. . . . Still, she was an unhappy creature, by the looks of her, and the evil she'd done didn't sit any too well on her. "It's all right," she said; "you can go on up."

Holy Mother, she thought, don't let the poor man be taken in again, him and his soft heart!

He was sitting in a rocking chair in Hermione's room; he was still a little thin, and his cough persisted. He had on a new dressing gown of imitation silk; Halys thought he looked strange and self-conscious in it. "Hello, Max," she said.

She didn't know what she'd expected, but not the warm look he gave her. "I'm glad to see you, Halys," he said.

She stood in the doorway staring at him; after a while a tear trickled down her cheek and she put out her tongue to catch it.

"Well, now," he said, "don't cry; there's nothing to cry about. Sit down; and I'll ask Hermione to make us some tea."

"You were always so good to me," she said tremulously. "I don't know why."

"Don't you?" he asked, and smiled. "I guess I couldn't help myself." But then he shook his head reproachfully. "You don't look very well," he said; "you don't look as though you'd been having a good time. I'm sorry for that; I thought when you left that you'd be happy."

"I am," she said. "I was." She looked at him piteously. "It's all my fault," she said. "I'm just no good."

"Tchk, tchk," said Max; he seemed to be genuinely distressed. "What has gone wrong?" he asked. "What's the matter?"

She shook her head, and looked at the floor. "It's

nothing," she said. "It's just that I can't go on. I have nothing to give him."

Max felt a coldness in his heart. "And Jon?" he asked. "What about him?"

"He'd be so much better off without me," she said. "I'm no good for him. I just hold him back."

"I see," said Max slowly; but he didn't see at all. There is a great deal here, he thought, which is under water like an iceberg. "Well, tell me," he said kindly; "why do you come to me?"

She swallowed once or twice; she seemed unable to come out with what she wanted to say. "I thought maybe if you took me back," she said at last in a frightened rush: "I mean—to live here, and work for you . . ." Her voice failed her, and she put her face in her hands and wept childishly.

Max got up and walked over to where she sat huddled in her chair; he put his hand out to touch her hair, and then drew it back again. "What kind of life is that?" he asked gently, "to live here and to work for me? Is that a dream for a young girl?

Is it from that that we get the great hopes we have for the young? Is that all you want for yourself?"

She answered, still not looking up, and in a muffled voice: "We could even . . . I mean, if you wanted to . . . I'd be willing . . . we could . . ."

He looked down at her with a curious expression. "I thought that you were in love with Jon," he said at last.

"Oh—Jon!" she cried, and wept afresh.

"I see," said Max, and turned away. He walked over to the window, and looked out; his expression was curiously peaceful, one would have said happy. "I was afraid perhaps you were not in love any more," he said. "But since that is not the case . . . come and live in the studio."

But now that it was offered to her, Halys drew back; she felt suddenly frightened; what was she doing? Perhaps after all . . . "I don't know," she murmured, distracted. "Do you mean you want me—"

"I want you to live in the studio," said Max

calmly, "and take care of it. But not for me." And as she glanced up at him in surprise, he added: "You will do it for Jon."

The red slowly stained her face as she struggled to make out his meaning. For Jon? Did that mean that Jon was to be there, too? "Do you mean both of us?" she asked uncertainly. "Jon and me, both? With you?"

Max shook his head, smiling. "No," he said, "not with me; I have other plans."

And he explained that he was going to live in Mrs. Bloemendal's house from then on. "I am to have a fine room with a north light," he said, "to use as a studio, so you and Jon can have the garage for yourselves. And I think that Hermione—Mrs. Loeb, that is, to be—will not charge any rent at first, so that he can get started with his lessons. And when she is not posing for me, she can teach you to cook."

"But why?" cried Halys, with her hands to her flushed cheeks; "why? When I acted the way I did?"

"Because," said Max simply, "the young must take from the old, they must take our places. The past, the future, neither can do without the other; so we move over to make room for you, and you should remember us, your teachers. So things continue, and it all goes on. Someday it will be your turn, there will be another tomorrow waiting, and Jon and I will both of us belong to yesterday.

"Do you know what is worst for the artist? It is to see young people with closed faces around him. Then he knows that nothing he has done has brought joy to anyone."

Halys rose slowly and a little unsteadily to her feet. "Can I tell Jon?" she asked. "Can I tell him now?"

"Why not?" said Max. "Run, do not walk. Tell him I will expect him for a lesson at half-past five, as usual. And tell him also to bring some wood, and we will all go to the beach for supper. I am doing another picture, of a woman, very tall, very erect, coming toward me across the sand . . ."

After Halys had left, Max went in search of Hermione. He found her downstairs in a little room off the kitchen, sewing away at a torn tablecloth. "You'd do better," he said after watching her for a while, "if you had remembered to thread your needle."

But, seeing how she kept her face averted, and how the color flooded her cheek, he added gently: "Were you so worried, Minnie?"

She nodded, still not looking at him. "I was afraid maybe you'd be sorry for her," she said at last. Her head drooped lower still. "I wouldn't blame you," she said, "if you'd wanted her back."

He came across the room then and knelt stiffly at her side and put his arm around her. "I have what I want," he said. "Let them be young for their own sake."

"You're sure of that?" she asked. "You're not just saying it?"

"For their sake," he said, "and for the sake of the miracle."

"And what would that be?"

"Why," he said, "the way young people come to love each other, year after year, here or in history, wherever they are. We're so accustomed to it that we never even give it a thought. But isn't it the one miracle of all that nobody can deny? to tell us what we have to know, that some power has us in exceeding care?"

"Is it love you mean?" she asked.

"What else?" he said. "What else can a man take into the dark with him, but the memory of it, old or young?

"There's a poem I learned once, long ago . . . if I remember it . . .

There is a Power, a Love, a Joy, a God
Which makes in mortal heart a brief abode . . .

Well, I've forgotten the rest. But what can I say to that Power, except 'Abide with me'?"

"Well, then, my dear," said Hermione, "I can't make you feel young again, no matter what I'd like."

He put his face down to hers, and felt her cool cheek against his own. "You make me like myself," he said, "the way I am; and that is all I need.

"Come along, now; I want to work on the torso while the light is right."

A NOTE ON THE AUTHOR

ROBERT NATHAN *was born in New York City in 1894, and was educated at private schools in the United States and Switzerland. While attending Harvard University he was an editor of the* Harvard Monthly, *in which his first stories and poems appeared.*

Except for two short periods during which he was a solicitor for a New York advertising firm and a teacher in the School of Journalism of New York University, Mr. Nathan devoted his time exclusively to writing. He is the author of some thirty-six volumes of poetry and prose, and from this body of distinguished work he has acquired a reputation as a master of satiric fantasy unique in American letters. He now lives in California with his wife.

April 1960

A NOTE ON THE TYPE AND PRODUCTION

The text of this book is set in Caledonia, a Linotype face designed by W. A. Dwiggins (1880-1956), who was responsible for so much that is good in contemporary book design. Though much of his early work was in advertising and he was the author of the standard volume Layout in Advertising, *Mr. Dwiggins later devoted his prolific talents to book typography and type design, and worked with great distinction in both fields. In addition to his designs for Caledonia, he created the Metro, Electra, and Eldorado series of type faces, as well as a number of experimental cuttings that have never been issued commercially.*

This book was composed, printed, and bound by H. Wolff, New York. The paper was made by P. H. Glatfelter Co., Spring Grove, Penn. Typography based on designs by W. A. Dwiggins.